A
Cure
for
Solitude

TLÖNBOOKS

David Whiteman was born in the Cotswolds in 1976.
He lived and worked in Prague before moving to London in 2001.
A Cure for Solitude is his first novel.

A
Cure
for
Solitude

a novel by **David Whiteman**

First published in 2008 by **Tlön Books Publishing Ltd** London

www.tlon.co.uk

Tlön Books Publishing Ltd is an independent publisher of books

Front cover and illustration © **Vishal Shah**
Typography by **Vishal Shah**

10 9 8 7 6 5 4 3 2 1

ISBN 978 0 9541468 5 6

Printed and bound in Great Britian by **Cox & Wyman**, Berkshire

A CIP record of this book is available from the British Library

For my parents.

'The question is the story itself, and whether or not it means something is not for the story to tell.'

Paul Auster *The New York Trilogy*

I

'So, what about you, Alex?'

The words don't sound like much but then it's his voice that gives them meaning. That only dawned on me when I heard him whisper those words for the tenth time in as many minutes. I soon began to wonder if they were just attempts at conversation, or was he doubting whether I had the nerve to go through with it? I had doubts myself.

At the time I had known him no more than a week. But even so, he could sense the panic that had consumed me since our first steps onto the plane. Although the plane was full but seemed so quiet. Knowing that we couldn't talk freely, I kept up the pretence that I was doing fine.

'So, what about you, Alex?' he said again, this time squeezing my knee.

'I'm fine,' I said. 'I'm fine, I'm just going to the bathroom.'

'Again?'

'My stomach won't stop turning. I told you I wasn't a very good flyer.' Any conviction in the tone of my voice was for the benefit of the passengers sitting near us. I had no hope of fooling him.

I made my way to the back of the plane, avoiding eye contact with anyone, supporting myself on the headrests of sleeping passengers. I closed the toilet door behind me, double-checked the lock and sat with my head in my hands. I was desperate to gain some control of my thoughts but it was beyond me. I sat helpless as my mind raced through the situation I had put myself in. With perhaps fifteen minutes before we landed I finally recognised this as a point of no return.

Reality and reason had absconded from my mind. I stood up from the toilet, placed my hands on either side of the basin and stared into the mirror. The fine hair on my temples was matted with sweat and cold to the touch. My eyes seemed more open than usual, transfixed by the horror of it all. I knew without saying a word that my voice had no comfort to offer me.

I tried to convince myself that he had faith in me and that that was all I had to remember. Whatever it was that he had seen in me was all it would take.

I splashed cold water onto my face to wash away the sweat and made some unnecessary adjustments to my hair. Trying to remember where the sleeping passengers' seats were, I made my way back to my own.

'Feel better?' he asked me.

'I'm sorry, Dominik,' I said. 'I didn't think I would get this bad.'

'It's ok,' he said. 'But now you are listen to me. Not your interruptions. It is something important.'

I ignored the captain's request to fasten my seatbelt and leaned towards Dominik. Understanding his accent is by no means hard, in fact it's a pleasure to listen to, but when reduced to a whisper, to catch every word, attention to detail is needed.

'First,' he said, 'when we are on plane, my name is not Dominik. You understand?'

'Sorry,' I said.

'Second. When we are leaving the plane, Alex, we are separating. Now, I go first and you must wait a short time before you follow. Don't try talk me, don't look me. No one should think we're together. Understand?'

There was a moment of contemplation before his words began to drum on my heart.

'No, I don't understand at all,' I said. 'You said you'd walk me through. We'd laugh and talk to calm my nerves, you said. Why the change of plan?'

I was having trouble keeping my voice to a whisper. Dominik had turned the plan on its head. As I understood it, we were to stroll through customs, chatting away and sticking together. We hadn't discussed every detail but he wanted us to give people the impression that we were tourists. He himself had likened the first smuggle to the first day of school. All nerves and brave faces and yet you get through it, one way or another. It had taken until now, I thought, but he had finally seen through me. I was going to get caught and Dominik knew it. It was time for him to wash his hands.

'It is not change of plan, Alex, it is change of tactics,' he said. 'You try to relax. I wait for you outside.'

He was expecting me to be delayed and in my mind it could only mean one thing. He tapped my knee and smiled.

'You'll be fine, Alex. You're a natural.'

The effort of trying to regain control of my thoughts, and taking in this supposedly innocuous change of plan caught up with me. I flopped back into my chair and closed my eyes. Dominik fastened his seatbelt and then mine as the plane began its descent into Prague. The thought that I might never set eyes on the city was the only one clear in my mind.

With my eyes still closed, the jolt of the landing was unexpected and disrupted what little peace I had found. Soon passengers began filing past my seat, walking towards the doors. Dominik fumbled around in the overhead compartment until he produced his small black rucksack. He quickly checked the side pocket for his passport and once he was satisfied he left me, joining the other passengers making their way off the plane. He made no attempts at any last-minute communication. Not even a harmless 'good luck'. I was on my own.

I counted to ten before making an effort to move. When I did I took my bag down and hung it over my shoulder, making it possible to keep my hands in my pockets. It didn't do much to stop them sweating, but it kept them out of sight. Dominik was long gone by now, so before I was the last one, I left the plane and followed the signs for the luggage carousel.

As I stood motionless, watching bags and suitcases that didn't belong to me, I caught sight of two guards. They weren't looking at me; I didn't know if they had already seen me. They were talking, but their manner didn't suggest that I was the topic of their conversation. It was merely the sight of their uniforms that quickened my pulse, and the golden reflections of light as the sun caught the black steel of their guns. I turned my attention back to the luggage, soon spotted my bag and walked up to meet it.

It was my hand luggage that was the danger if I was stopped and searched, so I contemplated stuffing it inside my bag. What use that would have been I can't tell you. It would only have alerted the guards. I decided I looked suspicious enough.

Dominik was five or six places ahead of me in the queue for passport control. I tried to catch his eye. I wanted to know if he felt the slightest sympathy for me. I prayed for him to at least acknowledge the ordeal, but nothing.

The passport official was certain to look at me if only to check my face against the photo. My skin was darker now and my hair a little longer. I knew that meant a prolonged look at my face. I would have to smile, I remember thinking. I couldn't keep a straight face for that long without looking guilty.

I never got the chance to act out my smile. The official was making it quite clear that he would rather be anywhere else than behind his desk. He took a quick glance at me before stamping my passport with all the grace of a robot and, handing it back, never said a word.

Through a set of sliding glass doors on the other side of the hall I could see Dominik, his hand beckoning me to get a move on. No sooner had I picked up my pace, the doors began to close. In the reflection I could see two guards behind me, quickening their pace and trying to catch up. One was talking into a radio, both were looking straight at me.

'Prosím,' said one of the guards. I knew he was addressing me but I kept walking.

'Prosím,' he repeated.

I knew I could plead ignorance to the request and back then my ignorance was genuine. I'm still not cured of it now. As I chanced a look at their reflection in the glass, to check on their progress, one of them caught my eye.

'Stop!' he called out.

The authority in his voice stopped me dead, almost mid-stride. One of them stopped by my side while the other walked around in front of me.

'You understand English, then,' he said, sarcastically.

'Yes, I am.'

'You are what?'

'I mean yes I do, but I am…English…sorry.'

I bit the inside of my lip and stared at their shoes.

'May I ask you the nature of your visit to Czech Republic?'

'I'm here on holiday.'

'You are alone?' he asked.

Over the guard's shoulder I could see Dominik on the other side of the doors. His thumbs were held aloft and he wore a grin that stretched from one side of his face to the other.

'Alone, Sir, are you on holiday alone?' repeated the guard.

'No,' I said. 'A friend is meeting me here.'

'And you're staying with this friend?'

'That's right.'

'Well, perhaps we can help you find this friend.'

He almost sounded boastful, as though his colleague ought to be taking notes on the masterful way he had backed me into a corner.

'That's alright,' I said, pointing to Dominik. 'He's already found me.'

Both of the guards looked to where I was pointing and I felt great satisfaction in watching Dominik's smile wither and die. It took a moment for him to straighten himself before replying with a tentative wave.

'No need for us to help you then,' said the guard.

He stood to one side and extended his arm towards the doors. I smiled and walked on. I would have liked to thank him for the offer of assistance but my mind was elsewhere. I longed for the throat of Dominik Rubin in my hands.

II

While Dominik bought a newspaper and some cigarettes at the newsstand I stepped out of the terminal and into the sunlight. I dropped my bags at the top of some steps, sat down and placed my head in my hands once again. The sun burned through my eyelids reducing the darkness I craved to a soft yellow haze. I had to think about my breathing while I waited for an onset of guilt, pride or sheer relief. I had no idea which it would be.

'Some of us are born with the luck.'

Dominik's arm wrapped itself around my shoulders and pulled my head down towards his chest. He let out a muffled cheer as he kissed the top of my head. I could smell a cigarette on his breath.

'Let's go home, Alex,' he said. 'Job well done.'

He stood in front of me and I looked up to try and meet his eyes but the sun sat squarely on his shoulders. All I could see was the silhouetted outline of his body, his neck extended towards me, inviting me to join the conversation. I lowered a bucketful of hope into the well of my mind in search of sense and understanding. The well was dry. I couldn't find words. I could not communicate.

Dominik picked up my bags as though it were some kind of reward, and made his way to the row of taxis parked at the side of the road. It was late May, but it was a dry, mid-summer heat, nothing like the weather I had been expecting; the sky was too blue and the clouds were too scarce. The day I arrived in Prague was the hottest of the year so far.

For the first ten minutes of the journey I thought we could have been anywhere. Our cab cruised over the same smooth tarmac roads you find all over Europe, so long as the money is there. But halfway into the city we hit the cobbled streets, and heavy vibrations came up through the back seat of the taxi accompanied by a deep, resounding hum. I sank into the corner of my seat, sheltering in the shadows from the sun, still awaiting the reaction that had eluded me so far. Dominik was talking to the driver, he sounded happy to be back home. I'd forgiven him by now. I sat silent in the back of the car just happy to still be free.

We began to cut through narrow streets and the buildings grew older, taller and dirtier as the heart of the city unfolded before me. I had never felt such a sense of familiarity with a foreign place than I did that day. It was like somewhere I had always dreamed of really did exist. A place to which I could always belong but never be lost in. They were nice impressions to have, my first impressions of Prague.

The taxi pulled up at the side of the road and Dominik settled the fare. The driver took our bags from the boot of the car and Dominik searched for his keys. I feasted my eyes on the street. Five-storey houses of yellow, pink and brown face out towards an avenue of delicate young trees and the stillness of the river. It didn't feel like a city at all.

'Come inside,' said Dominik. 'We're here. The land long promised.'

I bundled my way through the door, into the hallway and stopped at the cage to the lift. The lift shaft stretched up to the top of the building, wrapped in a spiral staircase that stopped one floor short of a domed skylight. It let in enough light to fill the entire hallway. It was beautiful, unlike any of the homes I'd had before.

'Well, call it down,' said Dominik, closing the front door behind him. 'Unless you take the stairs.'

Crammed together in the lift we ascended to the top floor. I saw that each floor had two front doors. As we passed each floor Dominik recited the names of the occupants, nodding to each door as he said their name, as though this were my formal introduction. On the top floor there was only one door, made with what looked like a thick, heavy oak. There was no name plaque like on the other doors, and no features apart from a small spy hole.

'So, who lives here then?' I asked, knowing the answer.

'We do,' replied Dominik.

It was his choice of words that first really endeared him to me. He makes you feel like you're a friend worth keeping.

After what seemed an endless operation with his keys, Dominik opened the door with a kick and I followed him inside. There was a large round wooden table that sat shining in the afternoon sun, with a vase of flowers, too dead for me to know what they were, or had once been, standing in the middle. At the far side of the room there were windows that looked out on to the river, as tall as any of the walls. The walls of the room itself were covered in books, alphabetically ordered.

'And I suppose you've read all of these,' I said sceptically.

'Reference,' he said. 'I am sorry for such a mess.'

I looked around and, although I knew where nothing really belonged, everything looked as though it was where it was for a reason and hadn't just been left or forgotten. Dominik looked sorrowfully at the vase on the table and took it through to the kitchen.

I strolled past the shelves with my head tilted to one side, skim-reading the spines of the books. I picked out the odd familiar word but most of the books were in a foreign language. I wondered if I hadn't completely underestimated the task I was facing.

'Don't worry,' said Dominik, coming back through. 'You don't have to read them all today.'

'Good,' I said. 'To be honest I can hardly keep my eyes open. You don't mind if I just sleep for a bit, do you?'

'No,' he said. 'You look like you should. I show you your room, but for the rest, you do your own exploring.'

Dominik took my bags and I followed him, again empty-handed, up a flight of wooden stairs that I hadn't even noticed. The stairs doubled back on themselves and led to a mezzanine from where I could survey the whole living room. It looked even larger than before, viewed from a height, but I was too tired to see anything new. A corridor led away from the mezzanine with doors on either side. I was paying little attention and just followed Dominik through the door he held open for me. He placed my bags down beside the single bed in the corner.

'I know,' he said, as if he had been listening to my thoughts. 'But we can do something with it. Make it look how you like it. As you know, I wasn't really expecting you.'

The room was plain, almost unfinished, not in keeping with the rest of the place.

Everything had happened so quickly that day that I hadn't had time to gather my thoughts. I'm sure I had a thousand questions to ask Dominik about what had happened that morning, but none of them occurred to me then. My mind was foggy with sleep.

Dominik made his way out of the room, pulling the door gently closed with both hands, as though I were a sleeping baby. I lay on the bed, nuzzled into the pillow and thought about nothing at all. It wasn't long before sleep came.

A few hours later I woke up to blackness, my mind as blank as my vision. I had slept so long that the sun had gone down and the only light in the room was that which spilled through the cracks around the door. After a few stretches on the bed I forced myself up and slowly walked towards the door, lifting my feet high off the ground, as I couldn't remember exactly where I'd left my bag. I opened the door just enough so that I could find the light switch. I found my bag, recovered some clothes and went to find Dominik.

At the end of the corridor I stopped on the mezzanine and, leaning over the banister, took in my surroundings again. Colours had changed and the character of the room had changed with them. The soft artificial light seemed to have shrunk it into a homelier size. Light brown wood sat against dark brown leather, and the countless books on the walls were lit by the light from brass oil lamps that I hadn't noticed before. It struck me as a room that lends itself well to thinking.

Dominik had taken one of the armchairs to the end of the room and turned it to face the window. He sat there with his feet on the sill, a drink in his hand and a cigarette held gently between his fingers, looking out towards the city.

'Why don't you join me?' he asked without looking round, instead addressing my reflection in the window. 'Come and see the view.'

I took a chair from the table, not wanting to disturb the peace by dragging another armchair all the way over. The vase had been returned to the middle of the table but was now empty, and the smell of furniture polish hung in the air. I put the chair down in front of the window, to face Dominik. He motioned his hand towards the window and checked with a glance to see where I was looking. Contented that I was taking in the view he shifted in his chair, looking for a little more comfort.

'It's strange place, you know,' he said once he'd settled. 'People are coming here for long time, some more welcome than others. Sometimes I think it is miracle the place is still here.'

Dominik pushed the butt of his cigarette into the ashtray that sat on the arm of his chair, then placed the ashtray on the floor beside him. His hand slowly strayed up, I'm sure without him knowing it, and began to stroke the crown of his head. His hair was very thin at the place where he stroked it. His scalp looked pale in contrast to the short dark hair that covered the rest of his head, from the tapered line on his neck to the widow's peak on his brow. It made him look more than a little monastic. His eyes had sunken since I had seen him last and the acute smell of alcohol came to me in waves as he breathed. He looked at me from the corner of his eye and I quickly turned back to the window.

I looked out onto a city that stands timeless. I thought that by now almost every city's skyline lay among the clouds, but the only buildings here that dared reach for the heavens were the spires of churches and cathedrals. Dominik talked me through the points of the city, following the river with his finger from as far right as we could see, to our far left, as the Vltava itself flows. Its dark waters reflected the lights that lit its banks. Old stone bridges, guarded by their weathered statues, reflected the artificial colours of night. And the clattering trams that crossed them burst with brilliant electric flashes of light as the sound of Europe softened from east to west. Nobody talks of Prague as a city divided by its river. The Vltava binds the city together.

'I think you like her,' said Dominik.

'She's beautiful,' I replied.

'Well, let us hope that she likes you.'

I waited until Dominik was ready to talk. I could tell his thoughts were elsewhere but I was unsure of the reason. It seemed that coming home had put him in a sombre mood, but then the plane ride itself couldn't have helped. Perhaps what had happened had given him a crisis of faith in me after all. This was when all the questions I hadn't been able to think of before came flooding into my mind.

'Dominik, why did you leave me on the plane?' I asked, concentrating on keeping the tone of my voice neutral. He shifted in his chair again and rubbed his face. Eventually he met my eyes with the same reassuring smile from the plane.

'You didn't give me any choice, I'm sorry,' he said. 'I thought we were both to be arrested.'

It wasn't the explanation I'd been hoping for.

'So you just left me to fend for myself?'

'It's not like that, let me finish,' he said, beginning to pay a little more attention to me. 'The way you acted on plane, the way stewardess was looking at you, it all looked... not so good. When you were in the toilet I took package from your bag and took it myself. That's why I left you. I had it.'

So, every emotion I had gone through that day had been born

of nothing. My achievement was nothing and my overwhelming relief had been, above all, completely unwarranted. The realisation left me feeling flat. Dominik's crisis of faith was surely a reality.

'I'll understand if you're having second thoughts,' I said in resignation.

'I'm not having second thoughts. I think you miss the point.'

'I don't see how,' I said.

'I underestimate you, that is the point. You have nerves on the plane today but there is not something wrong with that,' he said. 'All your nerves told to me today was that you are understanding the consequences of your actions. You knew what you were getting into. Only idiot would not have been scared.'

His voice slowly softened.

'If you get yourself into mess as you did today it's not unusual for customs to know about you before the plane touch to the ground.' Dominik placed his hand on his heart. 'I thought you were going to be stopped. That's why I took package.' He looked at me over the rim of his glass.

'You should have seen your face.'

We both smiled.

'But that's just it, you saw for yourself, I lost it.'

'No,' he said before finishing the last of his drink in one. 'What I saw today was promising apprentice. You thought you had the package, I thought customs knew who you are and you still walk away. And here you are now, free like the bird.'

He gripped on to my thigh, just above the knee, squeezed until I flinched and then let out the laugh he had apparently been bottling up since the airport.

'You're a natural.'

Dominik sprung out of his seat with an unexpected burst of energy. He crouched in front of me, took my head in his hands and kissed me on the forehead.

'Do not underestimate yourself,' he said.

He straightened himself, ruffled my hair and then walked towards the stairs.

'Come on, Alex,' he said, making his way up the stairs. 'You have to look lively.'

'What?'

'You're not going out dressed like that, are you?' He stopped on the mezzanine, where I had taken in the room just a few minutes before.

'Where are we going?' I asked.

'Out, my friend, and into the night.' He stood with his arms raised like a vampire bat. My spirits began to lift at his excitement.

'What for?' I called up to him.

Dominik spun on his heels and disappeared down the dark hall, leaving only his voice to fill the room. 'To celebrate, my friend…to celebrate.'

III

Our mutual friend was Lucy, although I wouldn't really call her a friend. Dominik and I haven't mentioned her since the day she introduced us.

I'd been back in London for about a month but neither had, nor felt, any real homecoming. My clothes lay strewn about the floor of the New Cross bed-sit I'd rented but I still considered my bag to be the place where they belonged. I had always planned to drop anchor in London, but, as a seabed, New Cross is made of brittle rock. The memories of a year in Australia and the slow crawl back through Asia were slow in fading. That month had been the longest of my life.

The friends I'd known before I'd gone away had moved on. They were busy carving out new and more fulfilling lives for themselves. I was trying to avoid the old and unfulfilling one I had shared with them, before I'd decided to travel. I felt as though fortune foresaw very little for me. The only thing I had in my life that was familiar and expected was poverty. That was at least dependable.

When my plane had descended into London it had been through a thick and blackened cloud that had somehow polluted my thoughts. The clouds didn't clear until Dominik blew them away.

On the morning I met him, Lucy had called to arrange a

time and place to meet. When I wrote my details in the back of her diary almost a year ago to that day, it never occurred to me that she might actually use them. But she had, and she had tracked me down. If her opening line hadn't been 'Hi Alex, it's Lucy. You remember me from the cruise?' I would have been struggling.

On the night of our date I sat on the bus for thirty minutes, to Kennington, where we were to meet, trying to salvage every scrap of information from the three or four conversations I could remember us having. We'd met on a sailing tour of the Whitsunday Islands which I'd decided would be worth reminiscing about. Other than that, all I could recall was a Canadian called Lucy who couldn't swim. One topic wasn't going to be enough to see the evening through. That's certainly why I was more receptive to the friend she had with her than I had been lately when meeting someone new.

We met in the Dog House on the corner of Kennington Road and Kennington Lane. I remember it being softly lit with candles on the tables and only half full. Almost perfect, although it had been Lucy's choice. I noticed her friend before I noticed her.

'Alex!' screamed Lucy, moments after I had walked through the door. She was dressed in defiance of the persistent drizzle outside. Lacerated jeans, a pink cropped top and a tired, blue tie-dye sarong wrapped around her shoulders. Her flip-flops clapped on the soles of her feet as she ran over to greet me. Her hair was dry from the sun. She didn't look like she'd been in the country for more than a day. She wrapped her arms around my waist and squeezed with everything she had. Using one arm to keep us firmly locked together at the waist, she leaned back and placed an open hand on my chest. 'Look at you,' she cried. She pinched my cheek, hugged me again and then prolonged a kiss on my lips. She was Lucy from Canada. She couldn't swim but she liked a drink. Things were coming back to me.

She took me by the hand and led me back to the table that she had sprung up from. I kept a tight grip of her hand, despite knowing that it might give her the wrong impression, as I was sure it would help her balance. Her friend stood up to be introduced to me, an effort that I found endearing. He was dressed expensively and mostly in black, which suited the colour of his skin. It looked stylish rather than morbid. Beneath the thick dark stubble that shadowed his face was an olive tan. I have never been good at guessing someone's age but I did well to place him at forty.

'Alex,' said Lucy. 'I want you to meet a very good friend of mine, Dominik. And Dominik, this is my very good friend,' Lucy paused for air and the faintest of giggles, 'Alex.'

We shook hands and exchanged a look which acknowledged Lucy's state.

'So, what about you, Alex?'

'Sorry?'

'How are you?' he explained.

I couldn't quite place his accent at first but I was certain it was European. He went to the bar for drinks, apparently so I could get the awkward pleasantries with Lucy over and done with in private.

Lucy as it happened was too excited for such pleasantries and launched into a rant about how good things would be, now that we were living so close to one another. Her lips were struggling with the number of words she tried to cram into each sentence, so her hands did their share of the talking.

Dominik returned with the drinks, two beers and a large red wine, and patiently waited for a pause from Lucy so that he could make a toast. Knowing that might take all night I raised my glass and caught his eye.

'Cheers, Dominik.'

'Yes, cheers,' he said, chinking my glass. We grinned at each other and both raised our glasses to Lucy. 'Cheers, Lucy,' we said in unison. We were happy to behave like children. Lucy raised her glass and nearly emptied it on the first visit. It seemed that another drink was all she was willing to stop talking for.

'So where did you two meet?' I asked them both out of genuine curiosity.

'Oh just here, a few hours ago,' said Lucy.

This put a very different light on things. Dominik hadn't made me feel as though I was cramping his style. I took it from that that I had been a welcome interruption. It amused me to picture the two of them together, Dominik now regretting whatever little plans he had been hatching.

'A few hours,' I said in surprise. 'I'm not late, am I?' Lucy closed her eyes and took a deep breath, as though thinking up some excuse for her early start.

'I had to meet a friend,' she said and then gazed at, or at least tried to focus on Dominik. Her forearms both lay flat on the table, more so for balance than effect, framing her glass. For a moment Dominik's face expressed some compassion but it concluded with a look of pity.

'I'll get some more drinks,' said Lucy.

Employing all the balance and concentration she could summon up, Lucy stood up from the table and made her way towards the bar. I followed her progress until I was sure she was safely there and then turned my attention back to the table. Dominik was sitting with his full glass raised.

'Drink up,' he said.

This was the first time we were solely in each other's company but I don't remember what was said. It might have been when he told me he was Czech, or perhaps he told me later. This is the moment that stays with me. There was nothing to suggest that our meeting was a matter of great coincidence, only in retrospect might it seem that way, now that we are what we are, but something did feel different. I felt as though our meeting was the fruit of inevitability.

'I don't believe this is happening,' said Lucy, back from the bar. 'It's so embarrassing.'

'What?' asked Dominik.

'They won't serve me. He says I've had enough.'

Lucy's cheeks were flushed and her eyes glazed over with

tears in the wings, awaiting their cue. Dominik laughed but I somehow managed to contain it.

'It's not funny,' wailed Lucy, she dropped her purse back onto the table in defeat and sat down.

She didn't exactly miss the chair but it somehow seemed to flip out from under her and came to rest at the nearest table. Lucy came to rest on the floor. Dominik laughed again, I cringed, and right on cue, Lucy's tears began to roll.

We didn't wait to be told we were no longer welcome. Dominik took his coat from the back of his chair and picked up Lucy's bag, leaving me to pick up Lucy. She didn't want to move at first but with some gentle encouragement she began to help herself to her feet. I wasn't the one who had got her into this state, but given how long the two of them had known each other, I assumed the responsibility for getting Lucy home fell to me. Dominik agreed emphatically and went to hail a cab.

He was standing by an open cab door by the time I got Lucy onto the street. I couldn't release my grip on her until we were both inside the taxi for fear that she would fall. Just as I was getting her head into a position that if she was sick it wouldn't be on me, Dominik told the driver the address and slapped the roof of the cab, having closed the door behind us. The taxi pulled out into the steady flow of traffic and when I turned to wave through the back window, as bright as the streetlights shone, I couldn't see Dominik anywhere.

'You're home!'

I shook Lucy's leg back and forth, repeating my words louder and louder each time, until my patience ran out. I walked around to her side of the cab and opened her door, catching her before she hit the road. I found myself having to support her and take my wallet from my back pocket at the same time. Eventually, getting the door shut, I dropped ten quid I couldn't afford through the passenger window.

By now, Lucy was making no effort to support herself so I slipped my arms through hers and began to drag her along. She lived in a three-story terrace with one bell on the door so I assumed whoever answered would know her. There was flickering from a television on the ground floor and I didn't want to look for her keys so I rang the bell. It played the theme from *2001: A Space Odyssey* and the tune was easily heard on our side of the door. It seemed to bring a little life back to Lucy.

Somebody fiddled with the locks and then a slight crack appeared in the door before the porch light came on.

'She's drunk, that's all,' I said, shrugging my shoulders. 'I thought I should see she got home alright.'

It was dark inside the house and with the porch light shining in my eyes it was hard to see who had opened the door. I could just make out a large, docile man on the other side of the threshold. The glowing tip of the cigarette protruding from his mouth slowly moved up and down as he nodded in agreement with me. Without saying a word he leant his head to one side and looked over my shoulder at the road. I turned to see the interest. Our taxi hadn't moved and its light was still out.

'Cheers,' said the guy who had opened the door. Lucy began to giggle uncontrollably as she was taken into the house. I waited until the door was closed and then walked down the path to the taxi. The driver was watching me, his arm resting on the open window with the engine still running.

'I'm walking from here, mate. I dropped a…'

'Your mate asked me to drop the lady off,' the driver interrupted, 'then take you back. It's paid for.'

He handed me back the ten-pound note I'd dropped through the window.

'Oh, right,' I said, a little flummoxed. 'Is he waiting for me?' I asked, but the driver just shrugged his shoulders.

When I went back into the Dog House I found Dominik sitting at a different table, further from the bar and close by the window. Again, he stood to greet me when I approached the table and again he shook my hand.

'I wasn't sure if you come. I thought perhaps you and the girl.' He grinned and raised his eyebrows.

'No, I don't think so,' I said.

'Very decent,' he said. 'I can buy you something to drink?'

'No, I'll get these. You got the taxi.' I felt in my pocket for the ten-pound note the taxi driver had given me. 'Same again?'

'Oh yes. I have a terrible thirst.'

I ordered two beers from the bar and they were the last drinks Dominik allowed me to pay for. The rest of the evening was spent, like most of our evenings have been since, with him unashamedly engineering the conversation.

He showed a genuine interest in me and a kind consideration for what I thought. I found myself thinking on the spot, expressing opinions I was unaware I had formed and, for the first time in what seemed a very long time, I was enjoying company and conversation again. I didn't appreciate how lonely I was until I met Dominik. Once he was in my life I was reluctant for him to leave it. But if I was only reluctant for him to leave, I was desperate for things not to go back to the way they had been. That's why I followed him to Prague.

That night the call for last orders rang like a schoolyard bell, calling an end to playtime. I racked my drunken brain for a casual reason as to why we should meet again, but he was way ahead of me.

'So, I tell you something,' said Dominik, getting to his feet and taking his coat from his chair. 'I have to go shopping tomorrow and buy present for friend. But, I don't know London so well. Maybe you help me?'

We made arrangements for the next day to meet in Trafalgar Square by one of the lions and go on from there. We said good-night and went our separate ways. On the way home I thought about the impression I must have made over the course of the evening. I thought it was a good one. I hadn't had so much to say in a long time.

IV

I woke up the next morning with a head heavy from the night before. The bus journey to Trafalgar Square did nothing to lighten it. In the sobering light of day I was questioning the good impression I thought I'd made on Dominik. Had he really shown such an interest in me, or was I just convenient company for the evening? Had I mattered to the conversation at all, or just provided the answers he'd expected? I didn't know anymore. Without any Lucy to break the ice and no Dutch courage, I imagined things would be slow to start with.

I couldn't see Dominik at any of the lions, but once I pulled myself up onto the plinth of Nelson's Column, to look down on the square, he wasn't hard to spot.

He stood by one of the fountains, as motionless as a statue, his arms outstretched as though he was being crucified. He was covered with pigeons. I stood there watching him for a moment, wondering whom the show was staged for; Dominik himself, me, or the crowd of mesmerised children who stood watching with looks on their faces that said they didn't know whether to clap or throw stones.

Dominik spotted me through the squint of his eyes and with one almighty roar of my name he sent the pigeons into a frenzy that in turn sent the children scattering. He walked over to me, waving his arms about, dispersing the last of the birds. He stood for a moment before speaking, brushing down the sleeves of his coat and laughing to himself.

'You're late,' he said. 'I had to keep myself amused.'

'And everyone else?' I asked.

I was far happier to see him than I'd expected to be.

Dominik raised his index finger and thought for a second.

'I can hear my stomach,' he said. 'It must be lunchtime.'

He insisted that we go somewhere the food was worth paying for. I had planned to buy him lunch but that didn't seem so likely now. We headed up St Martin's Lane and on to Covent Garden. I was still under the impression we had shopping to do. We talked as we walked but I don't remember what about; our concentration was taken up picking our way through the crowds.

We must have been their first customers of the day but, despite having the place to ourselves, Dominik chose a small table in the far corner, next to a plastic palm tree. The waiter had to take his newspaper to a different table so he could keep an eye on us.

Dominik ordered more food than I thought we could possibly eat, but I was wrong. He ate his way slowly and continuously through a soup starter, pasta main and side orders of salad and bread, occasionally making some comment about the taste of the food or how clean something was, but soon he resurrected the topics of conversation I thought we had exhausted the night before. He seemed to have some fixation with my future. It was a subject he never strayed too far from.

'So, Alex, where you see yourself, one year from now?' he asked, pushing his empty plate away, then reaching over for the small bowl of olives on the table next to us. It was as though he was giving me the opportunity to have the last word on all we'd been talking about.

'To be honest,' I said, 'in one year's time I would be happy to know what it is I want to do, never mind doing it.'

'I shouldn't worry,' said Dominik. 'I am sure that an unexpected opportunity will arise soon or later. It's only time.' I had no real idea of who Dominik was at this time and I wanted to know before I put too much faith in his words.

32

'What exactly is it that you do?'

'I'm a smuggler,' he said. There was no wink or tap of the nose, no finger to shush his lips. His face wore a blank expression I now know means: 'I have finished talking.'

'A smuggler,' I replied, as matter-of-fact as I could. 'That must pay well.'

'Well enough to buy you lunch,' he said, gesturing for the bill. But I didn't want him to be flippant. He must have expected me to question him or else he wouldn't have chosen to be so blunt.

'Do you always tell people what you do?' I asked.

'I don't think I am sitting here with you when everybody know my business.'

His tone made it clear he was having to state the obvious. I felt patronised. Obviously, my questions would have to be more insightful if I wanted any answers.

'So why tell me? Why am I different?'

'I don't know, Alex, I just get the strong feeling you are.'

Our waiter arrived with the bill. Dominik took out his wallet and, without checking the total, dropped a few notes onto the table as though he were littering. As we were both getting up to leave he caught my eye. 'You must meet me halfway on this, Alex,' he said.

It's not often that you meet someone without being swayed by a third party's opinion. As I said, I was, above all, lonely. I couldn't jump to negative conclusions about Dominik. At that point I wanted nothing more than a friend.

We ambled around the Garden for the rest of the afternoon. I asked him about Prague and he gladly answered my questions. We browsed through music shops. He asked me who I listened to and occasionally showed me an album to see if it met with my approval. I could see no theme in his tastes. We finished off the afternoon with a drink on one of the balconies that overlook the street entertainers. I felt cold and watched the cloudy sky for signs of rain. Dominik seemed to get quite into their acts.

The next day was Sunday, never the best day to need preoc-cupation. The promise that Dominik had made to ring me at some point was enough to confine me to my room all day.

The hours crawled by and the phone remained silent. I prolonged going to bed until about eleven o'clock. I sat up reading but wasn't really concentrating. I would read the same line two or three times before realising the words weren't sinking in. After ten minutes on the same page I threw the book to the other side of the room in a fit of impatience.

I lay down and stared into my bedside lamp for a minute, resenting myself for wasting the day. I looked at the hole in the wall that some previous tenant had stuffed full of old newspaper and painted over. I told myself, as I did most nights, that I should cover it up whether I was staying or not. Finally, I reached over and flicked off the light. At that moment, as though the wires in the building were cross-connected, the phone began to ring. From my bed to the phone my feet barely touched the floor. On the second ring I answered.

'Hello.'

'Will you meet me?'

'When?' I asked.

'Now.'

'Where?'

'Outside,' he replied.

I picked up the phone and carried it with me to the window by my bed. The street lights, most of which weren't working, gave off a dusky light. Just enough for me to register a distinct lack of life.

'Where are you?' I asked.

Dominik sighed.

'Outside, yes or no?' he repeated.

'Yes,' I said, and hung up the phone.

I threw on the same clothes I had not long discarded, locked the door behind me and descended the shabby stairwell to the street. I zipped my coat up to the top to keep out a drizzle so light it followed every twist of the breeze.

A long dark BMW pulled up on the opposite side of the road. Nobody got out, no windows opened and the engine kept running.

I didn't question who it was, just whether I should be getting in.

I kept my eyes fixed on the driver's window as I crossed, even though the glass was near impossible to see through. I opened the passenger door. Dominik was sitting behind the wheel tapping out a rhythm on his knees. I got into the car but didn't break the silence. He ran his thumb underneath his seat belt and slapped it back against his chest like a pair of braces. I took the hint and buckled up.

'Where are we going?' I asked.

He raised his hand to silence me and then checked the mirror. As the car gently pulled away the stereo came to life. I took the empty cassette case from the small shelf beneath the stereo. The sound of Vladimír Mišík's guitar filled the car, and his words, foreign to me, told stories I couldn't understand. The music was loud enough to keep conversation at bay.

Dominik turned left at the end of the street and, heading north, didn't stop accelerating, flying up through the gears, until he found a speed he was comfortable with. He didn't drive like someone who didn't know London so well. I sank back into the seat and closed my eyes. I thought through questions I might soon be facing but my thoughts kept turning back to the music.

As we approached Tower Bridge Dominik turned into a side road and parked the car. He suggested we take a walk. From the bridge I looked up to the floodlit towers. They stood bold and large against the sky with great authority, and seagulls swooned in and out of their shadows. When we were halfway across Dominik stopped, leaned onto the railings and stared down at the surface of the river.

'What's wrong, Dominik?' I asked. 'What are you so worried about?'

'Apprehensive, not worried,' he said, as though he were correcting my English. 'But I tell to you, you would have to meet me halfway.'

I wasn't as confused as I tried to look. I was sure I knew what he was going to ask me, but what little doubt I had was enough to keep me quiet.

35

'So, tell me, Alex,' he said, still staring down at the river. 'Have you ever been arrested?'

'No,' I replied.

'Then I would like you to come work with me,' he said. For the first time since we'd stepped on to the bridge he looked at me instead of the water.

'What would I do?' I asked, realising the appeal of the river's surface as a distraction.

'Nothing really, at first,' he replied. 'I'll teach you. I'll teach you what they teach me and then, if you like what you learn, we could work together.'

The Thames flowed beneath our feet, the lights of the Docklands shimmered on its surface and the traffic rumbled past behind us, but no distraction in the world seemed enough. I had no time to think.

'I'm not sure,' I said.

'Of course we'd have to go to Prague. Get away from here. The summer would probably be long enough. In winter, I imagine, we can be ready to travel.' Dominik's tone had turned quite light-hearted. 'And I'll pay you, of course, you won't need to worry about money.'

I didn't give Dominik his answer that night, although I could have. I told myself I needed time for the storm in my head to settle. I wanted to pick through the debris of information it would leave in its wake, consider my options, weigh up the pros and cons and arrive at a balanced decision.

Dominik drove me home and left me with his phone number. I didn't look back at the car as I crossed the street to my front door. I remember making tea and watching television. I don't remember sleeping.

V

I never did manage to weigh up the pros and cons. I didn't even try. All the things I stood to lose amounted to nothing. I couldn't be distracted from the opportunity to escape, to leave London, and above all, abandon the life I was leading. From the very moment Dominik mentioned it, Prague represented something precious to me. Hope.

It was early Tuesday afternoon when I phoned him. Dominik's number hadn't left the pocket of my jeans which themselves had hardly left my legs. I had barely slept since the proposition and there was no pattern to the sleep I had managed. It took a lot of concentration just to dial the number. Dominik answered his phone almost the second it rang. He agreed to meet me at a nearby pub so I could run through a few questions with him but I knew, and so did he, that I would give him the answer he wanted.

Afternoon sun broke through the pub's Venetian blinds, illuminating every speck of dust that hung in the air, and every trail of smoke that crossed the room. A barmaid soaked up the attention of two regulars who ignored the open pages of their newspapers. When Dominik arrived he found me sitting in the corner with a half drunk pint on the table. He was in a genial mood and it calmed my anxiety. He was dressed in brighter colours that day, maybe to influence or reflect his mood, but his stubble seemed to be a permanent fixture.

He bought two beers at the bar and then joined me at the table. He looked me in the eye and chinked my glass. He took a packet of cigarettes from his jacket pocket and lit one.

'So, what are these questions, Alex?' he asked.

'Have you ever asked anyone to do this before?'

'No, never,' he replied, and took a sip of his beer.

'Well, what about the risks? I've never broken the law before.'

'Everybody has broken the law sometime. People do it without thinking.'

'That's the point though. We'd be planning to. It makes a big difference to me.'

'That is why this is your decision,' he said. 'I don't make you do something you don't want to do. Ever.'

I had run out of intelligent questions and didn't want to ask any others. I wanted to be reassured that I was special and that he truly believed I was worthy of this gamble but, in between sips of his beer, Dominik just sat and waited to listen.

'Well, I've thought about what we talked about,' I said. 'And I'm going to say yes to your offer.'

'Good,' he said, and patted me on the shoulder. 'I have to go, Alex, I have busy day today. But I will see you tomorrow.' He finished his drink, stood up, took an envelope out from his jacket pocket and put it on the table in front of me.

'What's this?' I asked.

He left without saying another word.

As soon as Dominik was out of the door I picked up the envelope and opened it. Inside was a plane ticket to Prague, booked the day before, and a wedge of twenty–pound notes. I held the money underneath the table and counted it. There was one thousand pounds. The flight left from Heathrow at 1pm the following day. He had written his phone number inside the envelope. I sat there and began the drink that Dominik had bought for me. I had nowhere else to be.

VI

I booked a taxi to take me to the airport that morning. It took me less than an hour to pack. There were no last minute checks before I left and no contemplative moments at the door before it closed. I was glad to see the back of the place. Now it just seems like a low point on my continued travels. I don't really understand how I felt back then. I'm sure, however, that I didn't undertake the journey to Prague for the sake of the destination.

I hadn't rung Dominik that morning and we hadn't arranged a time or place to meet. I had decided to treat the flight as a test of my own commitment. I would board the flight with or without him and hope to see him on the plane.

After I checked in for the flight there was about an hour to go until boarding. The wooden front of the Shakespeare Bar promised a hideaway from the gleaming surfaces of Terminal Two. Dominik thought so too. He was sitting on the upper tier of a two-tier floor, quietly watching the television. There were two glasses of beer on his table, one untouched. 'Right on time, Alex,' he said as I approached the table. 'That's good start.'

'It's my first day at work. You have to impress the boss.' I pointed to the full glass on the table. 'May I?'

'Please,' he said looking pleased with both of us. 'We should eat,' he added, looking at the menu on the wall.

'It doesn't look up to your usual standards.'

'No, but it will be better than the shit on the plane.'

I smiled.

'You're probably right.'

Once we had eaten we walked to our gate. I kept close to him as we handed over our boarding passes. Once through, we were herded down some stairs and on to a waiting bus that drove us across the runway to our plane.

Dominik and I stood right at the back, gripping the handrails above us. He seemed to study the faces of the people on the bus, turned his back on them and leaned in close to whisper something to me.

'By the way, Alex,' he said softly. 'I hope you don't mind, but I put a little something in your bag.'

I gaped at him, waiting for a laugh or even a smirk to tell me that this was a joke.

'You don't mind?' he asked.

All I could do now was refuse to board the flight, which I thought at the very least would have got me searched and I didn't even know what they were going to find.

'It's a bit late now if I do mind, isn't it?' I said through gritted teeth. I could feel my hands going cold and I stared at the floor. My stomach seemed to be falling out from underneath me, taking on a life of its own.

'Lesson one, Alex. Never to panic.'

He smiled and patted my shoulder.

VII

Dominik had already drunk half a bottle of Becherovka on my first night in Prague but when we left the flat he seemed in reasonably good shape. We took the tram over the river, through the city to Náměstí Republiky, and walked from there. He was determined to celebrate and for this, by his reckoning, we needed champagne and a dance floor.

I'd never seen a club like the Roxy before. It was an old theatre with the seats taken out and some lights put in but nothing else seemed to have changed too much.

We stood watching the dance floor from one of the old boxes with a bottle of champagne on the table behind us and a full glass each in our hands. The atmosphere and heat coming up from the sweating horde of bodies beneath us was having quite an effect on Dominik and his determination to celebrate was beginning to rub off on me. The music was too loud to make easy conversation so whenever one of us spoke it was directly into the other's ear.

He'd had the nerve to accuse me of leering at the women.

'I was checking out the club!' I protested.

'Ah,' he said, rolling back his head. 'What is club if not the women?'

'The music?' I suggested, and he laughed loud enough for the people in the next box along to hear him. Not for a second did he think I might be serious.

It's probably my own lack of grace that makes me so fascinated with the way other people move. It's always taken alcohol and a lot of encouragement before I venture onto a dance floor. Dominik had gone to fetch another bottle of champagne. That's when I first saw her.

The rhythm of the music seemed to jerk the limbs of the other dancers as though they were puppets on the same piece of string but she was different. Some of them clapped their hands, some of them stamped their feet, some of them even punched the air but it was all to the beat of someone else's drum. She had thought in her every move. She orchestrated the music. It seemed to play in time to her body's movement.

I watched her all night but we didn't speak. She saw me looking once or twice but kept on dancing. I was drunk and content with my imaginary conversations that night, happy just to look.

Dominik kept himself entertained for the evening with the bar and the girls around it. Occasionally he would distract me with his forays onto the dance floor. Invariably with a bottle of champagne in his hand he would hop from one foot to the other while tossing his head back and forth. He looked like a tribal chief trying to summon the rain. I wasn't too sure whose drum it was that Dominik was dancing to, and judging by the looks on their faces, neither was anyone else. He seemed happy enough though, content to terrorise his own little corner.

With his dancing getting more chaotic as the night went on, it was only a matter of time before someone took a disliking to him. Eventually, a man in tight black jeans who had stripped to the waist, with long, sweat-soaked hair, gave Dominik a push in the chest. It wasn't overly aggressive but it was hard enough to get the attention of a few people nearby. They backed away when Dominik stopped abruptly in the middle of his rain dance and, unable to cope with the sudden change in movement, lost his balance. His legs buckled, he fell down onto his knees and then onto his hands. He stayed crouched on all fours like a dog, posing no threat, his head drooping down between his shoulders. The man in black jeans backed away and tried to lose himself in the crowd.

After observing Dominik's little incident I lost sight of the girl I'd watched dancing. I scoured the dance floor but she was gone. I wondered who with. There seemed no point in being there without her so I decided it was time to go. I went to fetch Dominik from the floor. He followed me outside willingly enough and never once objected to us leaving.

He had a strong instinct for bed that night, and while he made one last effort for the stairs, I dragged one of the chairs over to the window. I made myself comfortable and hoped I could stay awake long enough to catch sight of the sun. I wanted to see it flood the sky, and silhouette the towers of my beautiful city.

VIII

Every morning since my arrival I have dreamt of distant noises. The river breaking on the weir that stems from Kampa Island, the gentle clunk of the lift when it stops from floor to floor, or the passing rumble of a tram. These foreign sounds slowly fill up my head and all the space around me. I'm glad that my dreams incorporate these sounds. I see it as the safety net that cushions my fall back to earth, each and every morning.

My opinion on routine changed during the course of the summer. Now I see the benefits to a planned, efficient day with structure. I began to get used to my ideas changing. That has been a routine in itself.

'Routine, Alex, that is what we need,' Dominik informed me over breakfast on my first morning. 'Routine is the key.'

It's a phrase he repeats at least twice a day.

We awoke every morning at seven a.m. We didn't eat breakfast, we just had coffee. We would be up and out of the flat within twenty minutes. We would run for about an hour, sometimes more. It took me a while to build up to that but Dominik seemed comfortable whatever distance we ran. We usually headed out, away from the river; otherwise we'd have to run on cobbled streets. But we'd never run the same route twice, to try and get me familiar with my surroundings.

'Know your territory,' is another of his mottoes.

We were always back home by nine o'clock. From then until twelve, when we ate lunch, I suffered the most. For those three hours I would do one of two tasks. On a Monday, Wednesday and Friday it was the worse of the two: timetables. Dominik provided me with printouts of practically every timetable he could ever need. As long as it crosses a border he considers it relevant. The timetables are mostly rail and air routes in and around Europe, but he has American and Middle East timetables too, along with routes to and from every major shipping port in the world. It was my task three mornings a week to memorise times, destinations, connections, departures, airlines and their country of origin. I also had to learn time differences, daylight saving and travel times. Then, he insisted that I find out each country's peak holiday times, school holidays and all public holidays. This I had to find out for myself, as he didn't know them already, so, instead of committing these to memory, I recorded them and handed the notes over to Dominik for safe keeping. Lunch was always a relief. After lunch things got better.

He soon set about guiding me through the books that lined the walls. He selected books for me to read in the afternoon and then, when I'd finished at six, we would stroll along the banks of the river, in search of somewhere to eat. We became familiar faces in the restaurants on Kampa, particularly in the Fisherman's Club, where the smell of pan-fried carp and baked trout would drift out of the kitchen while we discussed what I'd read that day. Although I knew Dominik was keeping a check on my progress, the evenings never felt that way. We continued to enjoy each other's conversation as much as we had done from the start.

I read mostly literature and sometimes history. The literature was more often than not connected in some way to the period of history I'd been studying and, if not, I read Kafka. I felt at home in his stories.

I was working my way through text, absorbing information more deeply than I had ever done before. My brain was like a sponge, a long way from saturation. It was an education I'd never really had before. An education I craved for its own sake. When Dominik quizzed me over dinner, answers and solutions presented themselves to me with such ease I wondered where I'd found them.

On a Tuesday and a Thursday the only difference in the day was in the three hours before lunch. On these two days I studied Czech. Dominik would sit with me while I tried to learn but it was a slow process. Languages have never been my strong point but Czech was something else. Letters have different pronunciations, words have numerous endings and the grammar is still a mystery to me.

On Saturdays I would spend the morning looking at city maps from all over the world, trying to learn my way around their streets before I ever set foot on them. Saturday afternoons were spent in the pub, as was most of Sunday. Dominik might have suggested (he may even have believed) this was my reward for a hard week's work. I think it was for his benefit, not mine.

IX

The clock read seven a.m. as usual and the smell of freshly ground coffee gently awoke my sleeping senses.

We set out running at a gentle pace that morning, away from the river. Before we reached the streets of Malá Strana we took a left and zigzagged our way up the steep, grassy orchard on Petřín Hill, to a bird's-eye view of the city. When we reached the top, I stopped for a moment to catch my breath and leant against the wall that borders the park. I looked out at the city, aware that Dominik hadn't stopped running.

St Vitus Cathedral perched on the hill against the blue sky, the differing shades of the orchard's white blossom, the serpent Vltava slithering across a patchwork quilt of red rooftops. I could not read and memorize this, only see it and remember it less beautiful than it was.

I stretched out my legs and then set off again. Dominik was out of sight by now and I knew it would take me a while to catch him up. I always struggled for the first mile or two. As we approached the back of Prague Castle I saw him again and my sails began to catch their second wind.

'Dominik,' I called out, 'what made you so fit?'

'The army,' he replied.

It was hard to express any feeling with all my efforts concentrated on breathing. I wasn't really shocked about the army but he'd never been so direct before. I had a good idea of the knowledge that populated Dominik's mind but little understanding of how it came to be there.

'The army,' I repeated.

'You don't believe me?'

'I believe you. I just didn't think of you as the army type.'

'Neither did I, but the army didn't see it that way.'

I couldn't even begin to imagine a life in the army. I suppose, in some way, I had been living a military existence since I'd first arrived in the summer, but it was my choice. I was free to come and go and I didn't take orders.

'How long were you in the army for?' I asked.

'Until I ran away,' he replied.

He stopped running. We had reached the trees on the boundary of Letna Park and both stood in their shade. I crouched down to the floor, took a while to gather my thoughts and began to catch my breath again.

'So, where's your disguise?' I asked.

'You forget, Alex,' Dominik said, looking across the park with his hands on his hips, taking slow, deep breaths, 'this country have a new beginning. When I was in army we were just one more Soviet Republic. As their soldier, I served their cause, not Czech one. Nobody here is looking for me.'

'But who taught you how to smuggle?' I asked. 'They don't teach you that in the army.'

I stood up straight and Dominik put a hand on my shoulder.

'Well, an army of sorts,' he said. 'They taught me everything I know. They made me what I am.' He tapped his head with his finger. 'This can't be what they had in mind, but they are responsible,' he said. 'I am what they made me.'

He seemed to retreat inside himself for a moment. He took his hand away from my shoulder.

'Sometimes, Alex,' he said, 'you don't have the choice.'

'You always have a choice,' I said.

'Maybe in your world,' he said.

If I'd ever felt such compassion as I felt at that moment then

I'd never felt such longing to express it, but I didn't know how.

I closed my eyes.

'Crippled by communist regime,' said Dominik. 'What's your excuse?'

I didn't have one. To Dominik, I began to realise, our friendship was a forlorn attempt to extract some good from his life. I am twenty-four, what life have I had? One of us stood under the shade of those trees by choice, the other by circumstances beyond their control. Dominik put his arm around me and led me out of the shadows.

'Do you see that, Alex?' asked Dominik.

I could see the long black pole of the Letna metronome jutting into the sky.

'There used to be statue of Stalin there. But they blew it up, and now we have metronome that almost never works.'

'What does that mean?' I asked.

'I like to call it progress.'

Dominik smiled.

'Come on, Alex,' he said. 'We're running late.'

He checked his watch and rubbed his hands together, relishing the thought of whatever he had in mind.

'Now, I want you to close your eyes and use your imagination. Imagine running to our metronome that doesn't work. To left and to right there are steps that go down to road by the river. I want you to imagine the quickest way home, and then take it, as fast as you can. Make no mistake,' he added, 'this is a race.'

Dominik was silent for a moment to let me think. The streets of Prague twist and cross so often it makes judging the distance of your journey difficult, and which route is quickest near impossible. I settled on a route that I hoped would balance speed with the likelihood of me getting lost.

'Do you have it?' he asked.

'Yes.'

'Good,' he said. 'Now, you can't change your mind. You must stick to your plan and we see who gets home first.'

'I don't have a key,' I said.

'You're not going to win,' he replied.

Dominik raised his fist and took up a starting position. He extended a finger as he counted, one, two. There was no count of three. Instead, he was sprinting for the metronome, leaving only the sound of his laugh behind him.

X

I didn't have a clue where I was. I'd lost sight of Dominik about half an hour ago and I'd only counted on a twenty-minute journey home. From the bottom of the steps I'd made my way across the nearest bridge and towards the Jewish Cemetery. I knew, since I had to get to Smíchov, it was a stupid diversion but, for me, west of the river was relatively uncharted territory. My plan had been to cross the river and then, running against its flow, make my way back along the bank. I'd cross again at Charles Bridge and from there I knew my way home. At some point though I had lost the river.

I stopped running when I knew I was lost. Although the sky was still cloudless, the cobbled street on which I found myself was dark. I looked up at the buildings that crowded me. Cracked drains clung to the sides of the houses. They were four – sometimes five-stories high, and seemed to lean in towards each other. It made the darkness seem intentional. A thin layer of grime covered everything, as though it had seeped like sweat through the pores of the city. It marked my hand when I touched it, then stained my clothes when I tried to wipe my hand clean. Very suddenly it seemed quiet and I walked on, hoping that I would see someone soon.

I noticed how the walls seemed to sink beneath the ground rather than stand on top of it. I remembered what I'd read about the floods. How time and again, century after century, the river had spilled through the streets, into the churches and homes. So they built their city ever higher. Road on top of road, room on top of room. There was a world beneath this world. There was life beneath my feet. On the other side of the road a young boy disturbed the quiet. He was rummaging through a steel bin and dropping anything that took his interest onto the pavement. When he saw me he stopped what he was doing and began to cross the road towards me. His tatty clothes and his soft white skin were covered in the same grime that coated everything else. I slowly moved away. He said something to me that I couldn't understand and opened his arms, as though he wanted me to pick him up. I shook my head and kept moving, walking backwards. He kept coming. He tried to smile by baring his teeth but there was nothing in his eyes. I turned and ran.

At the end of the street I turned left and cut through a small square. I ran to the end of the opposite street and then I saw people again. They were on their way to work. There was no leisure in the way they walked. I was hot and sweaty from running again. I was still lost but at least I could feel the sun on the back of my neck.

At the crossroads where I found myself, no road looked the most likely to lead me back to the river. I realised I would have to ask for directions but I wasn't sure how. I stood at the side of the road and practised a few basic questions.

I shifted my weight from foot to foot. My feet were sore from the cobbles. I looked for a friendly face in the crowd and saw a young woman approaching. She was small and pretty, dressed smartly for work and wore flat-soled shoes. She was also wearing sunglasses, so making eye contact was out of the question. She looked young enough to speak English though and I was hoping for some sympathy if my Czech fell short of the mark. I stepped out into her path and smiled.

'Prosím vás, nevíte, kde je Vltava?' I said as rehearsed.

She stopped and looked up at me. I waited for her to remove her sunglasses but she didn't. I repeated the question. She didn't reply but this time she smiled. She lifted her glasses onto her head to hold back her hair.

'It's in Prague...isn't it?' she said.

'Is it that obvious?' I asked, a little put out by how easily she'd guessed.

'Yes,' she replied, 'it is. You watch me dance whole of the night and don't speak to me. You must be English.'

It was the first time I'd seen her since my first night in Prague. I had thought about her many times since then and now here she was standing before me, a figure that seemed indigenous to my imagination. I couldn't think what to say.

'So, take the left,' she said, pointing back behind her, 'and follow all of the people. You will find the river.'

I just stood there, wishing I wasn't sweating.

'You look like you're in the rush to find it,' she said.

'Ha...yes...I suppose I do,' I said.

She smiled.

'You don't speak much, do you?'

'I'm sorry, you just caught me by surprise, that's all.'

'Surprise see me or surprise I see you?' she asked.

'Oh God, both, all of them,' I said and laughed nervously. She laughed too but she was laughing at me. I didn't mind though. It even relaxed me a little.

'What's your name?' she asked.

'It's Alex.'

I offered my hand. The formality seemed to amuse her.

'Well, pleased to meet you, Alex,' she said and paused for a moment. 'My name is Olina.'

'Sorry,' I said. 'I should have asked. I'm not usually this slow.'

'It's OK,' she said, still smiling. 'No need to say sorry.'

'OK.'

Olina began to look through her bag. She found a pen and began to write on the back of a business card.

'So,' she said, 'you're not the only one who's in the rush but if you like, we can go out sometime.'

She handed me the card.

I took the card and tried not to look as surprised as I was. I briefly read what she had written. She'd spelt her name with an 'i' instead of the double 'e' she pronounced. I was glad to have read it after I'd heard it.

'I'll call you, I promise,' I said, holding up the card. 'Where would you like to go?'

'I leave it for you,' she said, 'but you don't like to dance?'

'Not really,' I said, 'but I don't know many places.'

'We'll find somewhere,' she said.

Olina began to walk away, continuing along the same path I'd stopped her in. Looking back over her shoulder she raised a hand to her ear, extending her thumb and little finger to imitate a phone. Then she waved, turned away and picked up her pace.

My shorts had pockets but none that I could trust with something so precious as her number. I carried her card in my hand all the way home.

I arrived back at the house about an hour after the race had begun. I'm not sure why, but on my way up to the flat I decided not to tell Dominik about Olina. We'd shared our lives for what suddenly seemed like a long time now but I wanted to keep this to myself. I liked things the way that they were. I told myself that's why I didn't tell him.

As the lift came to a stop I saw Dominik standing in the doorway, waiting to greet me and no doubt gloat.

'I don't know what route you took,' he said, 'but it was wrong one.' I stepped out of the lift and sent it back down to the ground floor. 'I think we can say I am winner.'

'It was a false start,' I said. 'Didn't you hear me calling you back?'

'No.'

He didn't stand to one side but I brushed past him into the flat regardless. The dining table gleamed and the flat looked tidier than it had for a long time. There was a strong smell of polish in the air.

'Where have you been?' he asked.

'I was lost, wasn't I. How am I supposed to know? I crossed

the bridge at the bottom of the steps and went right. I wanted to come back over Charles Bridge but it took me a while to find it.'

'You shouldn't have crossed the river at all,' said Dominik.

'I'll remember that for next time.'

'You should have known it for this time.'

Dominik closed the front door behind him and went to his desk in the corner of the living room. Before going upstairs to shower I started to select some books from the shelves. I was hoping he would forget the morning's Czech lesson as I was so late.

'Don't worry with the books today. Just go shower,' he said. 'You must go back into town.' This was unprecedented for a weekday. 'Why?' I asked.

'You need to buy some suits,' he said. 'I'm waiting for phone call but I think tomorrow maybe we will meet some people. Perhaps they have a job for us.'

'Tomorrow,' I said.

'Yes, tomorrow. Did you have another plan?'

I pulled a chair out from the dining table and sat down. I stared at my shoes.

'Are you sure I'm ready for this?' I asked.

'I think you've been ready for a while,' he replied. 'I just haven't wanted to disturb you, you've been working so well. Anyways,' he added, 'nothing's come up until now.'

I realised only then, in light of the things Dominik was saying, that I'd taken the comfort of my routine for granted and had lost sight of what I had come to Prague to do. In one of the dictionaries on the bookshelves I had found a definition of the word *apprentice: One who is bound to a master to learn the skills of an art or craft.* This was very much how I liked to think of myself and our relationship. On the surface. If he said it was time to move on then there was nothing to be gained by my arguing. Clearly, what I had to learn now was no longer in the pages of books.

'Perhaps we should take little holiday?' suggested Dominik.

'A holiday. Where to?' I asked.

'Dubá. I have small house in country. Not far from here, but far enough for holiday.'

'You have another house. Jesus Christ, Dominik, smuggling does pay well, doesn't it.'

'It's my family house,' he said, as though defending himself from an accusation of opulence.

'I didn't know you had a family, either.'

'I don't. But the house did…once.'

'Well, I'd like to go,' I replied.

'OK. After tomorrow. After tomorrow we go,' he said.

Standing in the shower, the water slowly heating the muscles in my back, I thought about Olina and our chance meeting. Before leaving the flat that morning I would have taken these sudden changes very differently. But meeting her that morning and the possibility of seeing her again enabled me to look from the outside in at all Dominik and I had been doing. He was no longer the only figure in my life now, and he wouldn't be able to mould me as he wanted with someone else's hands in the way.

I came downstairs from my shower to find Dominik packing a small overnight bag. He took some money from the top drawer of his desk along with his car keys. He put the money on the table.

'You need some new clothes,' he said, tapping the money. 'Don't be afraid to look smart. We go to Roztoky. I had my call.'

'Where are you going?' I asked.

'Dubá. I'll make it nice and clean.'

'Can I come with you?'

He just shook his head. He seemed unusually sullen and unwilling to talk.

'Buy a suit that fits you.'

'OK,' I replied.

'I will stay the night in Dubá.'

'When will I see you?'

'In the morning,' he said.

He took a jacket from the coat stand by the door and folded it over his arm. He took his bag from the table, hung it over his shoulder and smiled as he left the flat. He closed the door behind him as though it wasn't his.

XI

I lay on my bed with the card Olina had given me face down on my chest. I pictured the two of us sitting together and fabricated conversations we might have. I thought of the questions I'd most like her to ask me and rehearsed lucid, insightful answers.

Olina's phone number had ten digits whereas Dominik's only had six. I assumed this meant a mobile number. I had met Olina in the street that morning at about eight–thirty. She'd been on her way to work and, presuming she worked for eight hours, I guessed she'd be finished around five o'clock. The words printed on the reverse side of the card didn't make any sense to me. The only thing I was sure of was that my only chance to see her, without Dominik knowing, was that night. If I didn't ring her now I never would.

I took her number downstairs to the phone at the desk. I spent a little time clearing my throat and then testing my voice. I sat back in the chair, dialled her number, closed my eyes, counted the rings of her phone and braced myself for the sound of her voice.

'Prosím?'

'Olina,' I said, 'it's Alex, do you remember me?'

'Yes, of course,' she said, laughing.

'OK, silly question.'

'So, what it is?' she asked.

'Well, I hope you don't think I'm harassing you but something's come up. It looks as though I might be out of town for a few days, so, I might not get a chance to see you.'

'That's pity,' she said.

'Well, maybe we could have a drink tonight, before I go. What do you say?'

'I said that it's pity.'

'No, what do you say... to a drink?'

'I say yes,' she replied. 'Where do you want go?'

There wasn't the slightest trace of embarrassment in her voice.

'Well, like I said, I haven't been here long. I thought you might know somewhere.'

'To eat?' she asked.

'If you like.'

'OK, let's go Kozzy's. Do you know where is it?'

'I don't think so,' I replied.

'It's near the Old Town Square. So, you meet me before the statue?'

'Excellent,' I said, relieved to know which statue she was talking about. 'I'll meet you there. I'm looking forward to it.'

'Me also,' she said.

'Well, I'll see you then. Goodbye. Ahoy.'

'Alex,' said Olina.

'Yes.'

'How is seven o'clock?'

'Seven is fine,' I replied.

She said goodbye and I hung up to the sound of her laughing. I slammed the phone down on the desk and then slapped the front of my head. 'Wake up,' I yelled at myself.

I swivelled the chair around. I looked at the clock that hangs in the kitchen. It was twelve o'clock. I had suits to buy, and seven hours to be ready for dinner.

XII

I took a seat next to the statue and crossed my legs. I checked for dirt beneath my fingernails that I had cleaned not one hour ago.

Waiters working the cafes along the sides of the square sat at the tables they had attended to all day, smoking, catching the last drops of sun, and enjoying the calm before the evening rush. A few clusters of tourists strolled across the square making their way to the early evening concerts. Some briefly stopped at the town hall to puzzle over the astronomical clock.

I turned my attention to the statue itself. Stone figures lay all around the feet of one man who stood alone, looking across the square, weathered over all those years. I tried to imagine what it would take and what it would feel like to have a statue erected in your honour, what kind of life you must have to lead.

'Ladislav Šaloun,' said Olina. I jumped with fright.

'Where did you spring from?'

She smiled, glad that she'd taken me by surprise, and then looked back up at the statue.

'His name, Jan Hus,' she said, pointing at the standing figure.

'So who was the other guy?'

'Šaloun, he was the artist.'

'Oh,' I said. 'I never thought of that.' I stood up to join her.

'Nobody does,' she said.

We both stood facing the statue, Olina admiring the art

while I strained my eyes to the side, trying to see her without her seeing me. Her hair was tucked back behind her ears leaving a border of chestnut brown to frame her features. Her face shone as she smiled at the statue, the day's catch of sun still lying on the surface of her skin, not yet soaked in. 'So, what's his story then?' I asked.

'He was preacher against the Church... the crime Catholics. Before six hundred years! They burn him with the wood. How you say when you burn with the wood?'

'They burnt him at the stake?'

'Yes. They burn him with the wood stake.'

'Just like that?' I asked.

'It was big argument in Bohemia, like war. They put up statue before one hundred years.'

I wasn't sure what she was saying or how I was supposed to react to whatever it was she was trying to tell me. She spoke about it so matter-of-factly. She appeared to have information but no opinion of her own. I tried to think of an intelligent question that might show some understanding.

'Anyway, I'm hungry,' she said.

'Lead the way.'

'This way we go,' she said.

The walk took us out of the square and towards the river. I couldn't believe how quiet the streets were just a block away from the square. 'So, you found Vltava this morning?' she asked.

'Yes. You were right,' I said, 'it's in Prague.'

When we arrived at Kozzy's, Olina led me past the heavy damask curtain inside the door and downstairs to the cellar. It took my eyes a while to get used to the darkness, after the sunshine. I followed her through the room, past the long bar and a gathering of hard-drinking Czechs, past the candlelit tables, through an archway in the low brick wall to another room, and then, when she had seen every seat available, I followed her back the way we'd come to the most secluded table there was.

I took a seat and shuffled in my chair, trying to look busy and leaving Olina to speak with the waiter.

Dominik insisted I practice Czech on a regular basis. I'd mastered the linguistic basics of menus, bills and beer but that was where it ended. It's nice to know I won't starve but, as my pronunciation improved and my confidence increased, so did the frequency with which waiters attempted conversation, and it didn't take long to exhaust my vocabulary. The embarrassment didn't matter in front of Dominik but as far as Olina was concerned, it could wait.

'I order you the beer,' said Olina, lighting a cigarette. 'OK?'

'Of course it is.'

'I forget you speak good Czech.'

'What makes you think that?' I asked.

'This morning,' she replied, 'you speak very good.'

'I can say a few words but that's all,' I said, not wanting to get her hopes up. 'Anyone who wants a proper conversation can forget it.'

'I can't understand to you,' she said. 'You must speak more slower.'

'I said I can't really speak Czech.'

'Why you want to learn the Czech? Unless you want live here, and I wouldn't understand that.' She took a long draw on her cigarette as the waiter arrived with our beers.

'So, what you think the Czech food?' she asked.

'It's filling,' I said. Nothing else sprang to mind.

Olina smiled and exhaled, careful not to talk with smoke in her mouth. She said something to the waiter and he took out a note pad ready to take our order.

'You should have the fried cheese,' she said. 'You can't leave Prague without the fried cheese. It's not fancy but it's a good one.'

'How do you say it?' I asked.

She winked.

'I'll order,' she said. 'You will give to your tongue the injury.'

Olina said more than was necessary to order two meals and the waiter made her laugh with his reply. I felt like an idiot for not understanding and wanted to stop the two of them talking. The waiter picked up two menus from the table neither of us had read.

'So, you won't be needing these,' he said to me in very clear English. I picked up my glass and took a long drink of beer, pretending I hadn't heard him.

'So, what do you do, Alex? Why you in Prague?' Olina asked when the waiter had gone.

'I'm working for a man called Dominik at the moment,' I said, keeping my answer short. I didn't want to hand over, all in one go, the long-winded cover story I'd spent all afternoon preparing.

'And what do you do for him?'

'Dominik's into import and export. I pretty much do what he wants me to.'

'Are you trying to impress me?'

'OK, maybe it's not as simple as that but those are the basics,' I said. 'I still have a lot to learn.'

'You're the apprentice,' she said, surprised and pleased with herself at finding the word.

'That's me,' I said, wanting to close the subject. 'But what about you? Where were you off to in such a hurry this morning?'

'Hurry?'

'What do you do?'

'I work for travel agency,' she replied.

'That must be interesting,' I said.

'Not really. I spend whole of my days sending people around the world and I am stay at my desk.'

'Can't you find another job?'

'It's not my job. I think it's Prague that's problem.'

'But Prague is beautiful,' I protested.

'In winter, yes, but now it's not so pretty. There are so many tourists in summer. I can't see anything. Remember, Alex, I'm not so tall as you.'

Despite her joke I could recognise the tone of dislocation in her voice. I heard it in myself whenever I spoke, before I met Dominik. I couldn't help but sympathise.

'I know what you mean,' I said. 'I had the same trouble with London.'

'Is that where you're from?' she asked.

'I haven't lived there for a couple of years, but that's where I'm from. It's changed though,' I added. 'Too much for me.'

'Maybe you're the one who is changed,' she said.

'Maybe you're right, but it's easier to change where you are than it is to change yourself.'

'For you maybe, not for me.'

I was puzzled. Maybe there was something that kept her from leaving the city. A child that she hadn't mentioned, or something less complicated. She imitated the look on my face, reached into her bag and placed her passport on the table.

'It's not worth the piece of shit. I should give it to the bin.'

I reached across the table and took her passport. I flicked my way through to the thickest page, and smiled as I looked for her photograph. Olina grinned back at me and drew on her cigarette nonchalantly, knowing she had nothing to fear. The picture looked a few years old. Her hair was perhaps a little shorter but nothing that noticeable. There was nothing in it to poke fun at so I slowly picked through the pages. They were only noticeable for their lack of stamps. I handed the passport back, making every effort to look neither sorry nor surprised.

'I'm sure your's is better,' she said, putting the passport back into her bag.

'So where would you go if you could go anywhere?' I asked.

'Somewhere hot, I think.'

'Prague is hot.'

'Not for much longer. A paradise. A hot and tropical paradise.'

'Nowhere specific?' I asked.

'Reunion, perhaps. I'll show to you the pictures. It's beautiful.' She paused.

'Do you know why the ocean is blue?'

I thought it was a rhetorical question but she waited for an answer.

'No,' I said.

'It's a reflection of the sky,' she replied. 'And do you know why sky is blue?'

'Because it reflects the sea?' I guessed.

'Right,' said Olina. 'In Reunion, they're so blue it looks likes they're in love. Young loves, they only see the good in each other.'

'Is that true?'

She didn't answer but smiled, as though that were all the answer I should need. For the first time then I noticed her eyes. One was green and the other was blue. I couldn't see both colours at the same time. As my focus flitted from one to the other I began saying to myself – blue, green, blue...

'Anyhow,' she said, 'that's where I'd like to go.'

'You have a lovely turn of phrase,' I said.

'I'm trying to impress.'

'It's working,' I said.

She smiled. I smiled back. Green, blue, green...

'It's funny how we met,' she said.

'Yes, it's quite a coincidence.'

'What is coincidence?'

'When something that shouldn't happen, happens.'

'Why shouldn't we meet?' she asked, looking disappointed.

I took another sip of beer and thought carefully this time about what I was saying.

'Well, not that it shouldn't happen, it's just strange when it does.'

'Not really. Prague is small place. And strange.'

'I meant that it was good how we met. I'm glad that we did.'

'I think so, also,' she said.

I could see her disappointment when the waiter brought our food in the middle of the conversation. She said nothing to him bar *thank you*.

Although I had been in Prague some months already, that night felt like my first one in the city. I felt as though I'd been killing time since I'd arrived and that Olina was the real reason I was there. We shared the wine she had ordered with the meal. As the night wore on the colours of her eyes seemed to blend, until I could no longer tell one from the other, and my skin grew warm with the feeling of the wine inside me.

XIII

Prague wasn't as big as I'd imagined. It had only taken ten minutes after leaving Masarykova Nádraží before houses had begun to get bigger and further apart. The Vltava had swelled its banks and the hills had begun to grow steeper and greener. The trainline never wandered far from the riverside and my eyes never far from the window. The scenery wasn't breathtaking but it was captivating and new to me.

I sat opposite Dominik, shifting uncomfortably in the new black suit I had bought the day before. Whereas mine was clearly off-the-peg and hung like sackcloth from my shoulders, his navy blue single breast held him in an embrace.

'What did you do last night?' he asked.

'Just looked around,' I'd replied.

'You didn't go out?'

'Just for food.'

'So, where did you eat?' he kept on.

'Radegast.'

'You don't look too good.'

'Then I must have had one too many,' I shrugged.

When our train pulled into Roztoky my first impression was of the unique smell. Dominik pointed out that it was a local characteristic.

'I'm not sure what it is,' he said, stepping down onto the platform. 'It's been here as long as I can remember.'

I looked around to see if I could find the source of whatever it was that was hanging in the air. It was a sickly, chemical stench that, even when I think about it now, catches at the back of my throat. The sky was grey with low clouds and a small factory clung to the side of the hill that led to the town. The passengers who had alighted with us were the only people to be seen. Some put down their bags and checked their watches, while some began the steep climb home. I yawned, still suffering from a lack of sleep, but tried to inhale as little air as possible. Dominik was on the lookout.

'What did I tell you this morning?' he asked, turning around to face me.

'Straight ties make straight faces,' I said, as he adjusted my tie and slapped my face. A slight furrow of his brow told me that he didn't share my taste in suits.

'Let's go,' he said. 'Suley is here. He's a friend of mine. He take us to the meeting.'

I nodded, flattened my tie and followed Dominik. He led the way down the steps of the underpass. I dawdled nervously behind, repeating Suley's name so as to remember it.

Dominik stood at the main doors to the station, on the other side of the tracks, waiting for me to catch up. I was feeling rushed and wanted a moment to calm my growing nerves. With one hand on the door, he paused.

'You're nervous,' he said.

'I know.'

He put a firm hand on my shoulder and ushered me to one side, away from the door. I looked out of a window to the car park while Dominik rubbed at the balding crown of his head, waiting for the last frail old passenger to leave the station. He held the door open for her and she thanked him.

'You have no reason to feel this way,' he said. 'Today doesn't matter, I told you that.'

'It's just nerves,' I said. 'I'll be alright.'

'You be sure, Alex,' he said through gritted teeth. 'Nerves

are something but I don't want you sitting there sweating.'

'I'll be alright,' I repeated.

I was irritated at the suggestion I was going to go to pieces. I couldn't see that a few last-minute nerves were unreasonable. I wiped the palms of my hands down my jacket and took a deep breath.

'Let's just get on with it,' I said.

As soon as we stepped out of the doors Dominik threw his arms up into the air and strode across the car park to greet his friend. Suley was lifting himself from the bonnet of an old, silver Mercedes. The smooth brown skin of his head caught the light as it moved and, from across the car park, I could see his bush of a grey moustache. With his feet on the ground he straightened up. He was short, and his well-fed belly sat comfortably on top of his belt. Suley opened his arms, reflecting the smile I could picture on Dominik's face. He managed to let out a bearlike growl of affection before Dominik smothered him with a hug, lifted him a clear foot off the ground, and still their eyes didn't meet.

As slowly as possible I made my way towards the car. Dominik returned Suley's feet to the floor and I looked on as they greeted each other time and again. They looked like diplomats or world leaders putting on a show for the cameras but I didn't doubt their enthusiasm. Finally, Dominik turned to face me. I could see his lips beginning the introductions but I was still just out of earshot.

'...in London,' were the first words I caught, and then, 'Alex, this is my good friend Suley.' We took hold of each other's hand, 'And this is Alex.'

Suley thrashed my arm around for a few seconds in a frenzy of welcome and good wishes.

'Very pleased to meet you, Alex. It's always a pleasure to meet Dominik's friends,' he said.

'You've never met my friends before,' said Dominik.

'This is true,' Suley said. 'Maybe this is why I'm so pleased.'

'Nice to meet you, Suley,' I said.

He opened the passenger door and offered me the seat.

'Well, let us go. Dominik has probably told you, Alex, I don't like to be late.'

He smiled with reassurance that I knew all about him. It seemed inappropriate to let him know that, until our train had pulled in, I hadn't so much as heard his name.

'Of course,' I replied, getting into the car, 'we shouldn't be late.'

The road from the station snaked its way to the top of the hill and the livelier part of Roztoky. Suley took the straights as slowly as he took the corners, paying more attention to me than the road.

'You are from London. Dominik tells me so.'

'Yes. London, that's right.'

'Yes. I have friend in Brixton.'

'I know Brixton,' I replied.

'I have friends all over.' He took his hand from the wheel and made a circle in the air with the palm of his hand to represent *all over.* 'Every place.'

He returned his hand to the wheel and slowly pulled the car around the next hairpin.

'And me. Can you guess where I am from?'

I took this as an invitation to study his face more closely. I could only place his characteristics to a region, not a country. I didn't want to cause offence by guessing.

'East of here,' I said with confidence.

'Turkish, very good.'

'I've never been to Turkey. I'd like to go.'

'You will,' he replied, 'in this line of work.'

He winked and looked in the mirror. Dominik was silent in the back.

We reached the top of the hill. Many of the houses were more countrified than the city. But where there had once been land there were now concrete blocks of housing. After a slow slalom around the potholes in the road we pulled over. Suley twisted around in his seat until he was able to talk to us both.

'OK,' he said, 'let's get this done quickly. I'm really very hungry.'

'Is that all you think about?' asked Dominik.

'What else can I think about with an empty stomach?'

Dominik checked his watch.

'Are they here yet?' he asked.

'I can't tell,' replied Suley, looking out of the window. 'I don't know what they drive.'

Nobody suggested anything and I didn't dare speak. Suley shuffled back round in his seat and caught my eye.

'What do you think, Alex?' he asked.

'Maybe you should check,' I said. 'We don't want to be late.'

I appreciated the involvement. It seemed to settle my nerves.

'You're right, Alex,' said Suley. 'We'll be sitting here all day.'

'And you are hungry.'

'Yes, always hungry.'

He laughed as he turned himself around again to open the door. I watched him cross the street, pulling up his trousers as he went.

'We go back a long way,' Dominik said, watching him too.

'Why didn't you tell me about him before?' I asked.

'He gives better impression of himself. Better than I can do for him.'

He was right.

XIV

The meeting point was a pub but all that made it stand out from the nearby houses were a few garden benches, still damp from an early-morning shower. I hadn't taken my eyes off the door since Suley had gone in. Eventually he came back out onto the street.

'Watch his gait,' said Dominik.

There was nothing out of the ordinary about it. No limp or peculiarity.

'What's so special about it?' I asked.

'Nothing,' Dominik replied, 'but it's quick way to recognise someone. You should have the habit.'

Suley was back at the car before I'd had much chance to study it. He opened his door just a little.

'They're here,' he said. And just as on the plane, there were no last-minute instructions, nor words of assurance. Dominik followed Suley's lead, and I concentrated on Dominik's gait, just as a distraction. We entered the room one by one. Once we were all in, an old woman came out from the kitchen. She was pushing a rattling trolley stacked full of empty bottles. She carefully manoeuvred her way out through the front door and closed it behind her.

Harvest seemed to be the theme of the room with sheaves of wheat adorning the walls. An old wooden wheel, buckled and split, hung from the ceiling, covered in candles. Three men sat at a table just inside the door. There was a young man no older than twenty and two men in their forties. The youngest was dressed in jeans and what looked like an old white school shirt. He played nervously with a silver Zippo, flicking the lid open and shut. The other two were dressed in work clothes, farming or mechanics, it was difficult to tell. I felt overdressed. Suley spoke to the youngest in English.

'These are the gentlemen I have told you about,' he said.

He stood to greet us both then translated for the other two. I couldn't follow what he was saying, word for word, but I could tell it was Czech. I waited to see if Dominik would interrupt and speak to them directly but he said nothing. I promised myself I wouldn't speak unless spoken to. Suley took a seat at the head of the table, Dominik took a seat opposite our translator and I took the seat next to Dominik. I tried to appear as settled as I could. Dominik stared at the two elder men which seemed to make them restless.

'I won't bother with introductions, gentlemen,' said Suley. 'We won't be needing names. You have an offer you would like these gentlemen to consider?'

The two elder men insisted in having every word translated before the young man could speak to us. One of them spoke to him in such an exasperated tone that he must have been his father. The young man took the abuse calmly and thought before he spoke.

'We need your help, gentlemen,' he began. 'We have some business here in Prague but, also, small problem too.'

The moment he paused the two men wanted to know what had been said. I looked at Dominik, wishing he would just speak to them and hurry the whole thing up. He just stared ahead, listening to what was being said. The young man carried on flicking his lighter open and shut while he was being spoken to.

'Well, we all know the kind of help that's on offer,' interrupted Suley, 'so, let's get to the point.'

The young man raised a hand to the other two and they

stopped talking. He thought again for a moment before speaking.

'In two weeks we have delivery that must be moved very fast. But, we need papers, and now I told we cannot have. I get same papers in Berlin now but it take one weeks when everything ready but I can't keep delivery here. I need papers in Prague, day they be ready in Berlin.'

'Why don't you postpone delivery and get the papers your-self?' asked Dominik, breaking his silence in English.

'It too late. Delivery cannot wait.'

I noticed Dominik give Suley a quizzical look that I'd felt like giving myself. They weren't exactly playing their cards close to their chest. I couldn't understand it at all.

'What are these papers?' asked Dominik.

'Just passports… and things.'

'Things?'

The young man was forced to translate again. The other two had grown too agitated to be left in the dark for this long.

'We get the idea,' interrupted Suley, chairing the meeting once again. 'Perhaps we should talk about money.'

'Who pays, that's what I'd like to know,' added Dominik.

'We will pay you,' replied the young man.

'And who pays you?' Dominik persisted.

'It's complicated. However, we guarantee you get your money. We pay you.'

'But it's not your delivery.'

The young man glanced at his elders for a moment but got no response.

'No,' he replied, looking down at the floor like a guilty child. 'We just supply papers.'

'Not as things stand you don't,' I said.

I hadn't meant to say it out loud. Dominik glanced at me in amusement.

'We get nothing for lying to you,' said the young man, putting his hands together as though he were praying. The two elder men began to speak over the top of one another, growing more and more agitated, no doubt demanding some sort of explanation.

The young man spoke back and, not to his surprise, received an almighty slap on the side of his head from the man I was now certain was his father.

Suley covered his mouth with his hand but I could tell from his eyes how amused he was. I didn't know where to look. Dominik just sat there staring at each of them in turn while they continued to bicker.

'The reason I'm asking,' said Dominik, creating a respectful silence around the table, 'is because anyone involved with mafia should be paying good money.'

'I understand,' said the young man.

'And anyone smuggling people better know what they're doing.'

The original atmosphere of mutual curiosity, if not respect, had crumbled.

'Will you help us?' the young man asked.

Dominik looked at Suley and without saying a word, pushed his chair out from the table.

'We will let you know,' Suley said, and offered his hand to be shaken by the young man's father. 'We will be in touch,' he added, directly to both men.

I followed Dominik's lead and stood up from the table. We left Suley saying a few last pleasantries and went outside.

'How did I do?' I asked.

'Fine,' said Dominik, 'let's get in the car.'

He crossed the street mumbling to himself in Czech and let himself into the car, taking my seat in the front. I got into the back and kept quiet. Suley was following close behind us.

'So,' yelled Suley, starting the engine, 'what do you think of that?'

He slapped Dominik across the arm with the back of his hand and laughed from the pit of his stomach.

'I get you some interesting ones, don't I?'

'I'll tell you this,' said Dominik, 'there's no way I'm going to Berlin without some money first. They're a fucking joke.'

'Oh, don't worry about money. They've got plenty of that,'

said Suley. 'They're just in over their head, that's all. Perfect.'

'We'll see,' Dominik replied.

Suley turned the car around and headed back towards the hill. He and Dominik began to discuss where we should go for lunch. They didn't confer with me. Suley took the hairpins no faster than he had on the way up the hill. We had left Roztoky by the time they had finally agreed on somewhere to eat.

I sat in the back with my arm stretched out along the head-rests, tall and proud. It was my first time in a car since our taxi from the airport. Suley adjusted the rear view mirror trying to get a better look at me.

'And what does Alex think of our new friends?' he asked.

I looked at his eyes in the mirror.

'Fucking amateurs,' I replied.

XV

They decided on the Holešovica Kárkavána. I was hungry but Dominik assured me it was close by, sure to be open and, if the urge took him, Suley could treat us to some music on the piano.

Through the doors and down the steps we took a table near the bar. The place was modern and clean. Square black tables were placed like one half of a chessboard on a terracotta floor that seemed to squeal in pain whenever the legs of a chair moved along it.

Suley peered at the menu through, and then over, his newly donned glasses, as though the lenses didn't make the slightest bit of difference to his ability to read it. Finally, with a tut, and a shake of his head, he gave up and passed the menu to Dominik.

'Do you speak Czech, Alex?' asked Suley.

'No, not really,' I replied.

'This is not a mistake,' he said. 'It may be pleasant to the ears but it is not a pretty sight.'

Dominik, still busy with the menu, gave us both a tired look.

'Have you found me anything good?' Suley asked, leaning back into his chair while he kneaded and examined his stomach. 'I've lost weight since you last saw me, don't you think?'

Running his finger down the menu Dominik didn't look up. He just shook his head.

Eventually Dominik chose him something to eat. As usual,

I had to order. Beers for us, tea for Suley.

'Oh,' said Suley, once the waiter had finished taking our order, 'modest as well. You speak very good Czech.'

'Wait and see what comes,' I said.

While we waited for the food Dominik tried to find out all he could about the men we'd met in Roztoky, but Suley had more enthusiasm for sociable conversation. He wanted to know all about me. I wasn't sure where I stood with giving too much away so I kept my answers brief.

'London... we met in London... no, it's my first time... older than I look.' And so on.

Suley tried not to notice my evasiveness, but it spoilt what in other circumstances could have been a decent conversation. Dominik didn't see fit to help either of us out. I knew I was being tested by one, if not both of them, even if for no other reason than to see how much about myself I would give away, but it still felt uncomfortable. Our food and drink arrived quickly, to my relief. I'd ordered fried cheese, the same as I'd had the night before. That alone gave me some comfort. It was whilst we ate that Suley hit upon the idea of me going to Vienna.

'It's a very simple job, just right for you, Alex,' he explained.

Dominik put down his fork and swallowed.

'There's no such thing.'

'All I need is a lieutenant. Just for few days,' he explained to Dominik. Then he turned his attention to me.

'I need you to follow someone for me. You see, Alex, in three day's time, like our friends this morning, I'm expecting a delivery. A package. It should have been here, in Prague, yesterday, but someone made a mess. Now I'm told it's in Vienna and will come here by train. It's a very long and uninteresting story.'

'You'd rather we brought it back?' I asked.

'Oh yes, but it's too late for that. I just want you to follow it here.' Dominik nodded, apparently filling in the rest of the details for himself. It seemed this was a common practice.

Suley wasn't expecting his delivery at all. He wanted me, the lieutenant, to be there when these people crossed the border so that I could either corroborate or contradict any story that customs had intercepted them.

'It's really not very demanding. I think it would be the perfect little start for you, Alex.'

'Alex has already started,' said Dominik. 'We didn't come from London empty handed, did we?'

I smiled and shook my head, more in thanks than anything else.

'Even better,' said Suley. 'A man of experience.'

'Who are these people you can't trust?' asked Dominik.

'Is that important?' asked Suley.

'Russians?'

'Try not to overreact,' said Suley.

'Russians. I can't believe you're asking.'

There was no humour in his tone, just anger, and heartfelt disappointment. Suley sat still and quiet and perhaps a little embarrassed. Neither one seemed to know what to say to the other. Dominik was deep in thought, staring at his plate. It looked to me as if not far beneath his calm, cultivated surface lay an untapped reservoir of hatred. I didn't feel comfortable giving Suley an answer without Dominik's approval and I didn't dare to speak.

'Well, you can think about it, if you like,' said Suley, eventually. 'It would have been easy money, that's all.'

'What do you call easy money?' I asked.

'I hadn't really thought about it,' he said, 'but I'm sure we could work something out.'

Although I was excited I felt a little off-guard at the sudden mention of money. He could have quoted me the first figure that came into his head and I would have been clueless as to whether it was appropriate or not. Unexpectedly, Dominik spoke up.

'Two hundred and fifty thousand crowns. Alex will give you the answer tomorrow,' he said. 'Now, we please change the subject?'

For the rest of the day at least, that was the end of the matter. We stayed at the Kárkavána for the rest of the afternoon. At one point it felt as though dinner might have occurred quite naturally as a tail-end course of lunch. The two of them spent their time chatting, reminiscing and arguing about things I imagined neither of them cared much about. For the first hour I tried to look interested but as the afternoon drifted on, so did my mind. I had several daydreams that afternoon about Olina and all the things we could do with the money that was coming my way. I converted crowns into pounds and pounds into crowns and then back again. No matter where I stopped in the equations I was left with more money than I was sure could be right. In between sums I returned to thoughts of Olina. I imagined telling her how special she was. How, when I was back from my business in Vienna, I would take her away from Prague.

Suley began cracking his knuckles one by one. He picked up his coffee, took it over to the piano and placed it on top. He very slowly sat and lifted the lid. He played quietly with his right hand first and then gently with his left. His music was melancholic. Not like his persona but perhaps his nature. Dominik listened and slowly stroked the crown of his head.

Before long, Dominik took his wallet out and left more than enough money on the table to cover the bill. He looked at me and nodded towards the door. I pointed to Suley and shrugged my shoulders, not wanting to leave without saying goodbye but hesitant to interrupt. Dominik shook his head. We both stood, very careful not to move our chairs on the floor. We left him with his music.

I clutched the lapels of my suit together, sheltering from the chill of the late afternoon air. Through my buoyant and drunken eyes, I began to notice the signs of the changing season. Within a week the leaves had changed in colour and already most of them lay on the ground. They covered the streets and the parks of our walk home. Yellows and browns, golden and red, gathered together by people in places, thinly scattered by the wind elsewhere.

Dominik walked in front of me, looking up at the bare branches of trees as we passed them, silhouetted in the twilight.

I followed sluggishly behind, kicking my way through the leaves and following the traces of my breath in the cold air. I thought of the fire in the living room and then, folding my arms, I thought of my jacket that hung just inside the door.

When we were home, Dominik pottered about in the kitchen waiting for the kettle to boil. I was on my knees building a fire as quickly as I could, hoping to have the first flames flickering before he came through with the tea and started to interfere. He came in from the kitchen holding what looked to me like a biscuit tin and, sitting down next to the fireplace, began to rummage through it.

'What's in there?' I asked.

'Holiday money,' he replied.

'Who's going on holiday?' I asked, striking a match and gently guiding it towards the kindling and paper.

'I might have some shillings if you want them.'

I shuffled away from the fire and tried to rub some of the tiredness out of my eyes.

'Does that mean I'm going to Vienna?'

The kettle sounded from the kitchen. Dominik put the tin down in front of me and went through to the kitchen. He came back with the tea.

'Do you really think you're ready to go to Vienna?' he asked.

'What do you think?' I responded instinctively.

'It doesn't matter what I think,' he said. 'I'm not the one who's asked.'

'But surely you know better than I do if I'm ready or not.'

'Maybe, but if you can't make up the mind for yourself, then you can't be ready. Answer the question, you go or not?'

He seemed frustrated by the very idea of the trip. His tone gave it the weight of an ultimatum and now I felt as though I was being dared to go.

'Yes, I'm going,' I said.

'Good. I think so too,' said Dominik. We sat for a moment and watched the flames spread. 'I let Suley know tonight.'

XVI

The room was still dark when I woke to Dominik standing at the side of my bed, rocking me back and forth. For the second morning running, my head felt heavy from lack of sleep.

'Wakey, wakey,' he said.

'What are you doing?' I groaned, rubbing the sleep out of my eyes.

'You have busy day,' he said. 'That's all the sleep you get.'

He walked out of the room clapping his hands.

He'd aroused enough curiosity in me to awake my mind although I felt as though my body was still sleeping. I crawled out of my bed intending to return to it as quickly as I could and went to see what he was talking about. He must have been up for a while as the table was laid for breakfast. I could smell something frying in the kitchen. I took a seat at the table and turned to the window. The stars were clear but it was not night.

'What time is it?' I called through to the kitchen.

'It's six o'clock. I'd say you're late.'

'What are you talking about?'

Dominik came and stood at the doorway to the kitchen with a piece of toast in his hand.

'I spoke to Suley last night. He wants to see you.'

'Why?' I asked.

'He has to give you details for the job,' he said.

'You told him I'd do it?' I asked, awake all of a sudden.

'Yes,' he answered with a trace of amusement.

'When do I meet him?'

'St Vitus Cathedral. Seven o'clock. You must give yourself time to get there, so eat and get ready.' He took a bite of his toast and then busied himself with the coffee. He didn't seem in the mood for details.

I walked over to the window. A misty frame of condensation sat on each pane of glass. I wrapped my arms around me. There was just enough light to make out the white waters of the weir before Charles Bridge. Floodlights lit up the walls of the castle and within those walls stood St Vitus. High on the hill above the city.

'Why are we meeting at the cathedral?' I asked.

'He didn't say why.'

'Have you ever met him there?'

'No,' replied Dominik, putting two cups of coffee on the table. 'You won't come to any harm. The cathedral will be quiet at this time.'

I set out for St Vitus dressed for the cold with about thirty minutes to spare. I took a familiar route through Malá Strana, through Malostranské Náměstí and then up Nerudova towards the castle. I walked slowly, through empty streets and tried to clear my head.

I wandered past the iron gates to the castle, to an entrance at the left. Past the castle walls was a large courtyard. A Japanese couple sat by the fountain in the middle, holding each other. They looked as though the night before had not ended for them and they didn't look happy to see me. I walked over to a passageway on the other side of the court.

As I came out of the passageway my neck craned back, the enormity of the spire was visible for the first time. It was a Gothic tower of glass and gargoyles, frozen in one unnerving glare after the other.

I was standing not ten metres from the front doors but Suley was nowhere to be seen. My mouth had been dry since I'd left the flat. Now my stomach felt knotted too.

To the left of the main entrance a small wooden door stood ajar. In the small foyer was an unmanned booth and beyond it, through an archway, the belly of St Vitus. I slowly made my way inside.

Each step that I took on the tiled floor echoed. On the first step I paused. I followed the noise up from the ground and across the cathedral until it was swallowed by the mass of stillness. Then back it came, out of the stillness, as though something was imitating my movements. My feet were rooted to the floor. If I didn't move, I thought, no one would notice me. If I close my eyes, I told myself, no one could see me.

I slowly walked up the side of the cathedral to find the sanctuary of a pew and sunk down into the seat. Giant concrete pillars sprouted from the floor and soared up the walls until they forked and crisscrossed the length and breadth of the ceiling. Chapels and staircases lined the walls and the eyes of what felt like a thousand statues seemed to exert a physical weight on my mind.

Towards the main altar, I could see a statue of Christ. It was sculpted of gold and stood out clearly against the grey background of the walls. His arms were raised, ready to give a welcome embrace, but his eyes were lifeless.

I huddled down, out of sight, in my trench of wood. It was cold and I folded my arms together. I could hear voices behind me so I turned around as quietly as I could to see whose they were. The Japanese couple from the courtyard had followed me into the cathedral and were standing at the back. They looked up and admired the ceiling. The boy pointed to the altar and spoke. I could tell nothing from what he said. They each put an arm around one another and walked up the aisle side by side.

I lay down flat across the seat of my pew and closed my eyes. Either they wouldn't see me or they would, and most likely walk on by. I didn't care which so long as I didn't have to deal with them. I didn't care what they thought, who they thought I was or what they thought I was doing. I didn't know what I was doing.

When I had heard their voices pass I opened my eyes. I didn't think they had seen me. They hadn't stopped talking. I stared up at the ceiling and lay still, my fingers interlocked and my hands squeezed together. I could explain nothing to myself. Not why or how long I had been there. I breathed slowly and calmly, hoping my mind would follow my body's example.

I could hear the voices of the couple in the distance now. I gradually talked myself into moving and sneaked a look over the pew in front of me. It was only then that I remembered Suley. I looked around for him, hoping with all my heart that I wouldn't see him. I knew I had to leave.

I slid to the end of the pew. I watched the Japanese couple closely while I undid my shoelaces. They came to a plaque embedded in the floor and the boy attempted to read what was said. I took off my shoes, held them close to my chest and silently crept towards the outside world.

I stopped in the small foyer and put my shoes back on before stepping out into the light. A few clusters of tourists had gathered outside and were taking photographs. I wondered how long I'd been in there. I pulled up the collar of my jacket and buried myself as deep down inside it as I could. I hurried across the courtyard and back down the hill towards Malá Strana. The more distance I put between St Vitus and myself the better I felt. That glaring tower could probably see me every step of my journey home. I couldn't be sure because I never looked back.

XVII

You can hear the mechanics of the lift from every room in the flat when they're in action, but if he hadn't heard the lift he would have heard my keys in the door. Dominik was sat at his desk with the chair turned to face me the moment I walked in. As soon as he saw me he looked troubled.

'What have you done?' he asked. 'You look like you saw the ghost?'

'No, it's just cold,' I said.

'So, what happened?'

I walked over to the sofa and looked at the fireplace.

There was no trace of the ash from the night before.

'Can we light the fire?'

'The heating is on.'

'I can't get warm.'

Dominik stood up from the desk and walked towards me.

'How did it go with Suley?'

'He didn't show up,' I replied.

'Are you sure about it?'

'He wasn't there,' I replied without looking up. 'I can't get warm.'

I bent down to my knees and began to build a fire. It was an invaluable distraction.

'Are you sure you didn't have second thought?' asked Dominik.

'I was there but I didn't see Suley,' I said, slowly and as calmly as I could. It was a truth of sorts. I scrunched old sheets of newspaper into balls and laid them down on the grill.

'Do you still want to go?' he asked.

I picked up a handful of kindling and gently placed them down, one by one on the paper.

'You don't believe I showed up, do you?'

'I didn't say that,' he said.

'You didn't have to.'

Dominik raised his hand in defence. 'All I say is that before Suley calls…'

'I know what you're saying,' I interrupted, 'You're saying what you should have said last night. You don't think I can do it.'

'Alex…'

'No,' I shouted, 'thanks for the vote of confidence. It's just what I needed.' I threw the rest of my kindling into the fireplace, got to my feet and walked to the stairs.

'Calm down, Alex,' Dominik ordered.

'I am calm. You can tell Suley that I'll be in Vienna today. I'll let you know when I get there, so if he wants his job done, I suggest he rings me.' My voice tailed off as I heard myself issue an unplanned ultimatum. I turned my back on Dominik and walked up the stairs to my room.

'What if there is no job?' Dominik called after me.

'I'm going anyway.'

'But what for?'

I didn't answer him. I decided I needed to get out of the flat as soon as I could. It didn't feel like the sanctuary it had been before.

I packed a few things as quickly as I could. Enough for one or two nights. I put the shillings Dominik had given me the night before in my wallet. I had no idea what they could buy me. He was waiting for me when I went downstairs. He had finished building the fire and a thick blue smoke was billowing through the coals. He approached me as though I might turn and run like a startled animal.

'Take it,' he said.

He was offering me a mobile phone and a credit card. I took them and studied the card.

'You sign Harris,' he said, 'the name on the card.'

'I have a name.'

'It's more practical this way.'

I placed the card on the table and put the phone in my pocket.

'Then take some money.' He went to the kitchen to find his tin. He came back and pushed five hundred US dollars into my hand. I put it in my pocket and took my coat from the stand by the door.

'I will have Suley ring you. I promise.'

His assurance seemed like an apology on behalf of his friend. I couldn't bring myself to follow his lead of reconciliation. I picked up my bag and said goodbye.

XVIII

A feeling of vertigo had washed over me that morning and it still lingered. I had convinced myself it would persist until I left the city. I had found the address where Olina worked on the card she had given me. I desperately wanted to see her. She knew nothing of what I was doing and it made the prospect of her company all the more alluring. I needed to book myself on a train to Vienna, which gave me all the excuse I needed to see her.

Her office looked more like a waiting room at first glance. There were six members of staff, each sitting behind a high counter, and visible only from the nose up. I recognised Olina's frame of chestnut hair and went straight to her desk. She let out a little scream when she recognised me.

'I thought you are ringing me,' she said.

I couldn't answer her for a moment. I was still soaking up the beautiful normality of the situation.

'Hello,' she said.

I forced a grin as I tried to engage myself. I looked from one eye to the other, blue, green, blue. There was something in the way her green eye watched me that made me feel uneasy, as though it scoured me for imperfections.

'Are you OK, Alex?' she asked.

I concentrated on her soft blue eye and took a deep breath.

'I had to see you instead.'

'Really?'

'Yes. You see, I need someone with your expertise.'

'It is business or the pleasure, Sir?'

'A bit of both,' I said.

Olina raised her eyebrows and adjusted the angle of her computer screen, preparing herself for business.

'I need a train to Vienna,' I said.

'This is the business or the pleasure?'

'Strictly business.'

'Strictly business,' she imitated, poking fun at me. 'When you want go?'

'As soon as possible,' I said.

'How long you gone?'

She lifted her fingers off the keyboard.

'I'm not sure yet.'

'Are you coming back?' she asked.

I paused for a moment, pleased at the expression of anxiety in her face.

'Of course I'm coming back,' I replied.

If anyone else had asked me that question they might have got a different answer. But, even if my answer had been the same, I could not have given it with the same certainty I expressed to Olina.

She set about making arrangements for me. I would leave for Vienna that afternoon from Hlavní Nádraží, and on her recommendation, stay at the Maria Therisia. She made all the telephone calls for me. She spoke German with a great deal of confidence and it was calming to watch her do her everyday work. Eventually, with a ticket in my hand, I felt I had put the worst of the day behind me.

'When will I hear from you?' asked Olina, once all my details were clear to me.

'As soon as I'm back,' I said, 'I promise.'

She smiled and looked around at her colleagues to see which ones were watching then she stood up from her chair, leaned as far across the counter as she could and kissed me on the lips.

She sat back down immediately and smiled at me.

'Goodbye,' she said.

I left her office. The feeling of nausea that had been with me since St Vitus was no longer a serious threat, but my mind was far from settled. I wandered back through the old town, killing time until my train was due to leave. I came out by the river at Charles Square. A priest walked his dog while a number of white-collar workers sat eating an early lunch. Each had a bench to themselves. No one spoke to anyone else. I could see across the river to the street where I lived. The sun's reflection blazed on every pane of glass in the building. The avenue of trees I'd been so enamoured by on my first arrival now looked leafless and haunted. I turned away and crossed the square eager to catch my train.

XIX

The journey had gone by quickly and my state of mind had improved the greater the distance between Prague and myself. The train stopped regularly along the way, at small town stations. A father and young daughter sat opposite me in our chosen carriage. He held her up to the window and encouraged her to read the name on the sign at each stop, but she grew frustrated and tired as the journey went on. The sun went down over thick forest and distant, tremulous lights began to appear on the darkening landscape. When we arrived at their stop, he had to carry their bag while she slept on his shoulder. I watched him kiss a woman on the platform who took the bag from him and I nearly cried.

I took a cab from the station to Maria Therisia. I'd never been to Vienna before but I felt no desire to explore the place. The thought of leaving the hotel grounds and forgoing my status as a paying guest didn't appeal. It was my mental state that needed attention and not the city beyond the hotel doors.

I unpacked my things as soon as I was in my room. I laid them out on a chair where I could see them and climbed onto the bed. I probably lay there for a couple of hours, I don't really remember. When I woke up I splashed some cold water on my face and changed my shirt. I was ready to face the bar.

There was nothing intricate about the interior of the hotel.

It was modern and modest and required no concentration to navigate, for which I was thankful. The round, pine bar shone brightly from its latest polish and sat neatly in the middle of a featureless room. The barman was standing in the moat between the bar and a castle of glass, mirrors and bottles of booze. He polished a large wine glass with the white apron tied around his waist. And, he didn't seem happy, until, when held up to the light for inspection, the glass was so clean it all but disappeared from view.

A couple sat together in the corner contentedly ignoring their drinks, and there were two solitary drinkers at the bar. They were seated as far apart from one another as possible, one at twelve o'clock, the other at six. I pulled out a stool in between them and ordered a glass of beer.

I drank the first one quickly and ordered another right away. I had nothing to read, no one to talk to and nothing that came to mind that I actually wanted to think about. It didn't take long before what appeared to be the drunker of the two men slowly began to worm his way off his stool. I could tell that he was on his way to talk to me. He tried all the while coming over to catch my eye. I gazed vacantly into my beer, postponing as long as I could the inevitable.

'Hey, if you're trying to drink your troubles away, you're going to need something with a little more... punch.'

He threw a slow-motion punch and pressed his fist into the top of my arm. His voice was gravelly and his words a little slurred. There was a copper-tinted drink in his glass and on his breath. He didn't feel it necessary to wait for an invitation. Beckoning the barman over he hauled himself up onto the stool beside me. He pointed down into his glass, winked and raised two fingers, apparently intent that the transaction should be done without saying a word.

'My name's Patrick, by the way,' he said to me.

'Alex,' I replied. I could hear bottles being displaced on the other side of the bar. 'What are we drinking?' I asked.

'English, I knew it!' cried Patrick, leaning one arm on the bar to safeguard his balance. His eyelids had lowered to half cover his eyes. They looked weighed down by alcohol. He seemed undecided whether it was worth the effort that it took to keep them open. 'I could tell you were English the second I set eyes on you,' he said, sounding very pleased with himself.

'I had to wait for you to open your mouth before I could tell you were American.'

I finished my last inch of beer and picked up my new drink the barman had just delivered.

'So what brings you to Vienna then, Alex?' asked Patrick, trying to sound sober and serious.

'I had a few days off work so I thought I'd have a change of scenery,' I said.

'And what's the usual scenery?' he asked.

'Prague.'

'No shit!' Patrick sprang up and doubled the attention he was paying to the conversation. 'Me too, I haven't seen you around before, have I?'

I laughed into my glass.

'Why would you have?' I asked.

Despite there being over a million people in Prague, he looked as though he found it genuinely strange that two of us had never met before.

'I don't know…I just thought…so you don't work there.'

'Yes, I just don't go out much.'

It felt as though I was trying to offer an excuse for my absence. Perhaps we should have met. How would I know? I'd been living what no one else would consider a normal life under Dominik's constant watch. I'd been blinkered all that time to any social distractions the city might have offered. Patrick began to reel off the regular bars and clubs he and his friends frequented. I counted in disbelief as I continually shook my head in response. I hadn't heard of one.

'You've got to get out more. That ain't healthy.'

'Well, I've had a lot of work on lately, but maybe…'

'Maybe what?' Patrick asked.

'I'm not sure. Maybe I'll get some free time soon.'

'Work's getting slow?' he said, a premature sympathy in his voice.

'No,' I replied. 'It just has to change.'

I had to steer the conversation for a while as Patrick made the usual enquiries about work. It didn't seem difficult. I no longer surprised myself with the ease at which I lied, but I impressed myself immensely.

It wasn't far into the conversation that it occurred to me Patrick was the first person I had met since leaving England who would claim English to be his mother tongue. I had never got the impression that Dominik thought I was holding anything back from him when we talked, but talking to Patrick was noticeably different. It didn't put me on my guard but instead loosened my tongue. His understanding gave me access to a range of words I'd not used in so long I was no longer one hundred percent sure of their meaning. But that didn't stop me talking. Anyway, Patrick was hardly in a state to argue over the merits or meaning of my words.

The drinks kept coming and I kept drinking them. I don't remember how long we sat there or much of what we talked about. I tried to concentrate on the answers Patrick gave to the questions I asked him, but his answers were long and slow and went in broken circles. By the time he got within touching distance of the original question he had forgotten his point.

As we talked my mind drifted back from Olina to Dominik, to the morning in St Vitus, and for the first time in months, back to London, and what might have happened if I'd stayed. Unconnected thoughts would chase through my head until a hot flush would rise up inside me, occasionally bringing with it the taste of vomit. This would be my cue to focus once more on Patrick's narrative and try to pick up where I'd left him. As the night wore on he spoke in ever-decreasing circles, so it was never long before he came around again to the same subject.

While trying to pay attention to him, I became aware of a sensation in my crotch. Somewhere between my skin and the bunched layers of my trousers it felt as if something had begun to leak. I tipped back off the stool and, stumbling for balance, I looked down expecting to see a wet patch spreading down my trouser leg. The sensation stopped and then came again. I began to scrabble in my pocket for the vibrating phone.

'Hello?' I said.

'Hello, where are you?' I recognised Dominik's voice without thinking about it.

'Hold on,' I said. My shock reaction to the phone had attracted everyone's attention. I excused myself to Patrick and took the phone into the toilet.

'I forgot to call. Sorry.'

'That's OK. Where are you staying?'

'I can't remember. It's a name like a...'

I came across a sign bragging about the cleanliness of their toilets on headed paper.

'Maria Therisia,' I said confidently. 'That's it.'

'Exactly how drunk are you?'

'I'm not drunk.'

'You sound drunk,' said Dominik.

'I'm alright,' I snapped.

I could picture him on the other end of the line, shaking his head and cursing the decision to let me out of his sight, believing that it had been his decision.

'Well, anyways,' he said in a calm voice, 'you should get some sleep. Suley will call you in the morning. You should be ready when he call.'

'What time?' I asked.

'I'm not sure. Early. He wanted to call tonight but I won't give to him the number now. You need a clear head when you speak to him.'

He paused, giving me time to cross his words but I couldn't. The last thing I wanted was Suley ringing with a list of details I would have to commit to memory.

'But you don't know what time?' I asked.

'In the morning. I'll call you first.'

Familiar warmth had crept back into his voice. A soft tone that I had missed. Either he hadn't used it or I just hadn't heard it since the morning of the meeting in Roztoky.

'Alex, you are alright?' he asked. I could tell he wouldn't be brushed off with a flippant answer.

'Yes,' I said as sincerely as I could, 'I'm alright.'

'Well, goodnight. And go to bed.'

He hung up before me.

Patrick was still at the bar but he was using it as a backrest now as he slouched on his stool, his glass dangling from his fingers. I didn't want to drink any more. Dominik's concern had left me feeling guilty and I knew that one more taste of vomit in the back of my throat wouldn't be kept down. Patrick straightened up when he saw me.

'I'm going to bed,' I told him bluntly, hoping that the message wouldn't take forever to get through.

'One for the road,' he protested.

'No, really, I'm going now.' I didn't want it to turn into a debate but surprisingly Patrick didn't seem to mind.

'OK,' he said, 'but you can't leave this.' He reached behind him and passed me what was left of my drink. 'It was nice meeting you.'

I took the glass from his hand and chinked it against his. He made a toast to new friends and, if that was all it took to get myself to bed, I'd drink to that. We exchanged a nod and finished our drinks.

A goodnight and a brief handshake later I was free to go to my room. I carefully made my way out of the bar and down the hall towards the lift, concentrating on trying to walk in as straight a line as possible, keeping my eyes focused on the lift door.

I made the mistake of glancing down at the carpet, and after that it became almost impossible to focus on anything. It seemed to wobble slightly, then the red paisley pattern began to move, different shades and colours swirling and blending with each other, the sound of the bar behind me, warped and frantic.

I lunged for the lift and began hitting the button to call it down. I could feel gravity abandoning the contents of my stomach and an almighty storm being unleashed in my head. My knees jerked in and out of position as I tried to stay upright, then, losing control, I turned around, leaned against the wall and slid to the floor. A thick sheet of darkness was crawling out from the corners of my eyes. I felt as though I was sinking into the carpet. I raised my head as though to stop myself from drowning. Through the small hole of what vision I had left I could see Patrick. His face was blurred and shapeless like a watercolour. He was stretching his neck and adjusting his tie, walking tall, quickly and formally. I just registered his arms, stretching out towards me, before my final bubble of perception burst. I was left with what I see now. The infinite blackness of space.

XX

VIENNA

'One of the leading hotels in the Austrian K & K chain, the spacious Maria Therisia offers modern comfort in historic surroundings. Set in the ancient artists' quarter, this stylish hotel is within easy walking distance of most of Vienna's sights, making it an ideal base from which to take in this beautiful city. Location...'

'Alright Peter,' said Konstantin, 'that's enough.'

The room was in darkness and when Peter wasn't talking it was also very quiet. Peter placed the hotel brochure back onto the coffee table. He stopped the recording, rewound the tape and listened back to the sound of his own voice.

'Just once,' Konstantin muttered to himself, 'I'd like to be a paying guest.'

He walked up and down the room, in and out of the shadows, scuffing his shoes on the carpet. Thinking of the long night ahead, he broke the promise he'd made to himself and opened the door to the mini bar. He browsed the shelves and the trays inside, his face illuminated by the light from the fridge. He made a mental note of each brand of spirit, how many bottles there were, and how many he could risk stealing.

'Why do you insist on torturing yourself?' Peter asked, speaking into the microphone clipped to his lapel.

He got no answer. Konstantin was still devoting his attention to the mini bar. Peter rewound the tape, listened back through his headphones and checked the levels again. It was a mindless routine that stemmed from extreme boredom, and one he had carried out many times over the years.

Konstantin closed the fridge door to shield himself from temptation and the room was dark again. He walked over to the French windows and tried to force them open. He sighed in exasperation when the latch would not yield.

'I would die for a cigarette,' he said.

Peter sat quietly in his chair in the corner of the room, unable to understand all the fuss. For Konstantin the wait was unbearable.

'There's a window in the bathroom,' Peter said, leaning over to rewind his tape by force of habit. 'Smoke in there.'

'I can't. He'll smell it. He smells everything.'

The door to the room rattled on its hinges under the force of someone knocking. Konstantin ran to the door. He made a brief check through the spyglass and, seeing whom he'd expected to see, hurriedly opened the door and stepped to one side. Peter stood to greet the new arrival.

'Good evening, Mr Grechko,' said Peter.

'Sit down,' Grechko said, striding into the room. 'I don't want you getting dizzy.'

'No, Sir,' Peter said, sitting down obligingly.

Grechko made his way across the room and over to the French windows. There was a click in the latch before he rolled back the heavy glass door and stepped out onto the balcony.

Outside on the balcony Grechko lit a cigarette. He followed the traces of smoke from his mouth, trying to pinpoint the moment they became remnants of breath expelled from the pit of his lung. He pulled at the grey strands of beard that sheltered his skin in the cold evening air.

Peter and Konstantin waited inside, one more patiently than the other.

From his bag Peter took a pack of cards.

'Do you want a game?' he asked.

'I can't concentrate now,' said Konstantin. 'Why do you never suggest it at work?'

'This is work,' replied Peter.

'I haven't got money to give away.'

'Then we won't play for money.'

There was a knock on the door, only this time more gentle. Konstantin checked through the spy hole once more then opened the door.

'Come on in,' Grechko called from the balcony. 'Come and smoke my cigarettes.'

Peter watched the man walk over to the balcony. He wore a suit with no tie and a long dark jacket. He placed his black leather bag on the bed, removed his glasses to clean them and acknowledged Peter's presence with a nod. He stepped out into the cold and took a cigarette from Grechko's open packet. He lit his cigarette, took a shallow drag and shivered.

'My God, it's colder than Moscow.'

'Prettier too,' said Grechko.

'How about this for retirement? You could build a pretty little house in the country.'

'Who can afford to retire,' replied Grechko.

He took another cigarette from his packet and lit it with the smouldering butt of his last.

'I hear that they took out your lung.'

'So,' replied Grechko, 'I have one left. How many do I need?'

'You shouldn't be smoking.'

'I asked for a doctor, not a nurse,' Grechko said, and took another heavy drag on his cigarette.

'So, have you finally found him?' asked the Doctor.

'Not yet,' Grechko said, shaking his head. 'All the time we're getting closer but we're not there yet.'

'You mean *you're* not there yet. You're the only one who has ever cared.'

Grechko glanced at the Doctor. He stepped forward and bent over to rest his arms on the wall of the balcony.

'I don't expect they could even tell you who he is,' the Doctor said, looking back over his shoulder into the room.

'That's not the point,' said Grechko.

'So what is the point? Only you would know.'

Grechko didn't answer, he had grown tired of the conversation. Every time the two of them had it, it seemed to grow shorter. These days there was barely anything left of it.

'So what do you want to know?' asked the Doctor.

'Everything. I want to know everything that he knows.'

'Where is he?'

'Downstairs. He'll be up soon.'

'If he's drunk you'll have to sift through it,' said the Doctor. 'He won't shut up.'

'I said I wanted to know everything,' insisted Grechko.

'I'm just saying, we could be here all night.'

Grechko flicked his cigarette over the balcony.

'Fine,' he said.

Somebody coughed to seek attention and Grechko turned round. Konstantin was standing at the window.

'What?' asked Grechko.

'They're on their way up.'

The Doctor dropped his cigarette over the balcony and followed Grechko back inside. He took his bag from the bed over to the window where there was more light. He unpacked his things, laying them out in the order he would use them while the others waited in the hall. Cleansing solution first, cotton wool last.

Grechko watched the numbers above the door to the lift as it ascended. Peter watched up and down the hall.

'Konstantin, go back inside,' said Grechko. 'You're crowding the hallway.'

Anxious to find a use for himself Konstantin stood just inside the door to the room, ready to close it once the others were safely inside. He heard the bell of the lift, then footsteps coming down the hall. One by one bodies filed into the room. When the last body was in, Konstantin closed the door behind them and switched on the light.

'Keep it off. What do we need it for?' snapped Grechko.

Konstantin hit the switch again as fast as he could. He turned and strained his eyes to see what he could in the darkness.

Peter was checking the tape machine one last time while the Doctor was assembling his syringe. Standing in the middle of the room and breathing heavily was a slim built gentleman dressed in a suit and tie. Draped over his shoulder was the unconscious body of a young man, no older than twenty-five, thought Konstantin, whose weight had clearly become a strain to the other. With Gechko's help the gentleman carefully placed the body into a chair.

'On the bed,' the Doctor said, scornfully, holding his syringe aloft. 'How can I stick it in his arse if he's sitting on it?'

Grechko and Peter took one arm each and dragged the body over to the bed. Peter pulled and twisted at the young man's belt, eventually getting the trousers down to his knees. The others stood back and watched with a sense of unease. All except the Doctor. He rolled the young man onto his hip and bared a small area of flesh. He chose his spot and wiped it clean. He squirted a small jet of solution into the air to remove any air from the needle and injected. The skin hardly resisted as the needle sank into the muscle. The Doctor breathed deeply as he forced the solution into the body. When the syringe was empty he gently pulled the needle free. A small drop of blood seeped from the skin and he held a ball of cotton wool to the perforation.

'Give it just a minute,' he said.

When the Doctor was finished Peter rolled the young man onto his back and went to fetch the recorder. As far as he was concerned his shift was over. Someone else could move the body from now on.

Konstantin took his place and helped Grechko lug the young man back to the chair. They held him upright while the Doctor placed a mask over the young man's eyes.

'Can you hear me, Alex?' asked the Doctor.

He repeated the question time and time again as Peter fixed the microphone onto Alex's shirt. Grechko and Konstantin slowly loosened their grips as Alex began to support his own body weight.

'I can hear you,' said Alex.

Grechko released his grip on Alex altogether and clenched his fists in excitement. As quickly and quietly as he could, he moved around from behind the chair and took a seat next to the Doctor.

'That's good, Alex,' said the Doctor. 'If you can hear me that means I can hear you. If I can hear you, Alex, I can find you. Do you want me to find you, Alex?'

'Yes.'

'Yes what?'

'Yes please,' Alex mumbled drowsily.

'Do you want me to find you, Alex? I'm losing you, Alex,' the Doctor said loudly. 'You have to keep talking, Alex. Can you hear me?'

Alex could hear a distant voice drifting in and out of coherence.

'Where are you, Alex?'

'I'm here,' he replied.

Alex's head slowly dropped. The Doctor took him by the shoulders. Grechko stepped forward and smacked him hard on the side of the head.

'Keep talking!'

'Where are you, Alex?' the Doctor demanded again.

'I'm here, I'm here,' cried Alex. 'Don't lose me!'

The legs of the chair clattered on the floor as Alex rocked back and forth into a frenzy, desperate to be heard.

'I'm here,' said the Doctor. 'I can hear you.'

He waited while Alex slowly calmed his frantic breathing.

'I'm coming to get you, Alex, but you'll have to keep on talking.'

'What should I say?' Alex asked, timidly.

'Tell me about yourself, Alex. And your friend, Pavel. Tell me all about him.'

'I don't know anyone called Pavel.'

'The man that you work for.'

'Dominik,' said Alex.

'Your friend Dominik,' said the Doctor. 'Tell me about your friend, Dominik.'

'What do you want to know?' asked Alex.

'Everything, everything you know. You just have to keep on talking.'

Alex leant back into his chair and seemed to relax.

'Tell me the things he tells you, Alex. What does he say?'

'So, what about you, Alex?' he said, to the voice in the darkness. 'The words don't sound like much but then it's his voice that gives them meaning.'

XXI

The sheets on the bed lay evenly flat either side of his body, as though he hadn't moved a muscle in his sleep. The mobile was ringing on the bedside table. He had the feeling that wasn't the first time he'd heard it that morning. He stretched across and answered the phone.

'Hello?'

'So, what about you, Alex?' asked Dominik. 'How's your head?'

Sitting up in bed, Alex looked around his unfamiliar hotel room, trying to recollect the night before.

'It's that bad is it?' Dominik asked, having heard no reply.

'No, it's not that bad actually,' said Alex. 'What is it?'

'I said I would call.'

'Did you?'

'You don't remember?'

'What time is it?' asked Alex.

'It is half hour before Suley is going to call you. I suggest you get up and get ready. This job is today. Are you coming back?'

'It's ten o'clock,' said Alex, surprised to see his watch sitting on the bedside table. It wasn't a habit of his to take it off at night.

'Yes,' said Dominik, 'so, you'd better get up.'

Dominik had been encouraged by the few words of reconciliation they had exchanged the night before, but Alex seemed oblivious to whatever had been said. Hung-over and irritable, it wouldn't take much for a rift to reappear. Dominik spoke gently.

'I'll see you tonight then?'

'Yes, I'll see you tonight,' Alex said, staring at his clothes, piled on the chair. The phone went dead.

Still incapable of remembering how he had got to his bed, Alex threw back the sheets and left it. He fetched a bottle of water from the mini bar and took it out to the balcony. He took a long drink of water and, in the hope that it would revive him, bared the cold breeze on his skin.

XXII

DUBÁ, CZECHOSLOVAKIA, 1988

'Oh my God,' she said.

'What?'

'Pavel, you have to look.'

He was too far from her corner of the loft to see what she'd discovered so he got to his feet. His legs felt sore from having been crossed for so long. He shook them to restore some feeling in his knees and, watching for his head on the beams of wood, walked over to his sister. Her arm stretched out to meet him before he was half way there, a photo in her hand.

'I can hardly tell the difference looking at you now,' she said, shaking her head. 'It has to be Dad or it wouldn't be up here but just look at him, look at the two of you. It's unbelievable.'

Pavel looked long and hard at his father's features as a young man. He studied the prominent bones that shaped his face, the hook of his nose, the creases around his eyes, and the scars just visible on his skin. He was so marked for one so young.

'I have more hair than that, Martina,' said Pavel.

'For now, maybe, but that's not my point,' she said. 'Look at him. You look like twins!'

True enough, he thought. The photo was like his reflection.

Their father stood alone at the gate to his garden, smiling broadly and facing the camera. He was wearing old work clothes that he lived in all weekend and his hands were black with soil.

The path in the background, which led to the only road to the village, was as overgrown then as it still was now. Neither of them could remember the photo being taken but the location, they agreed, was unmistakable.

He handed the photo back to Martina and she returned it to the empty space in the album. It was hard for Pavel to tell these days if he had any real memories of his father. He suspected that the ones he had were just the product of his imagination, ignited by pictures he'd seen, or stories he'd been told. He watched over her shoulder while she flicked through the pages of the album.

'Was that the door,' she asked, 'or did I imagine it again?'

'No,' replied Pavel, 'I think that time it was.'

Martina placed the album back in the chest where she had found it, stood up, picked a path through the boxes that lay scattered across the floor and carefully lowered herself onto the ladder.

'Don't fall,' Pavel called, waiting until she'd reached the bottom. It was an old childhood habit.

He knelt down for a closer look at Martina's discovery. Nothing in the chest looked immediately familiar to Pavel, which hardly surprised him. He could not remember how many years it had been since he had last ventured up to the loft. He'd never imagined there was much to find. His mother had never struck him as a sentimentalist before and, until now, never a hoarder either.

The chest was mostly full of old clothes. Men's jackets and crumpled trousers. Perhaps, he thought, in their day, they had carried the scent of the man she loved more potently than anything else, making them impossible to part with. They smelt of nothing to him, at least nothing that stirred his memory.

Resting on top of the clothes was the photo album Martina had been studying and, next to it, an old shoebox. The lid was missing and inside Pavel could see a collection of old money, badges, and a stack of small sealed envelopes held together with string. He picked them up and untied the string. His father's name was written on each one but there were no addresses. He wondered how long they had sat there, their ink fading, waiting to pass on their message.

'Pavel,' he heard Martina call.

He didn't answer.

'Pavel!' he heard her shout again.

'Yes?'

He returned the envelopes to their box and walked to the top of the ladder.

'It's Mrs Vanová,' Martina whispered, once she had her brother in sight. 'She's come to see how we are.'

Pavel came down the ladder and followed his sister into the living room. Mrs Vanová got to her feet as soon as he entered the room. She was slim and elegant but looked elderly compared to his memories of her. Her hair was white, her eyes had sunken and there seemed so little flesh on her hands. She clutched a handkerchief to her mouth.

'Good afternoon, Mrs Vanová. How are you?' asked Pavel.

His gentle words were all that was needed to break her frail self-control and reduce her to tears. She buried her face in Pavel's chest and cried.

'I'll put the kettle on,' Martina said, making an escape to the kitchen.

'I'm so sorry, Pavel,' Mrs Vanová said, once she'd composed herself. 'I must be the last thing you need at a time like this. Just ignore me.'

'Don't be ridiculous,' Pavel said, ushering her to a chair. 'You've had as big a shock as any of us. And you're as welcome here as you've always been.'

Mrs Vanová perched on the edge of the deep sunken chair by the fireplace.

'She looked very peaceful when I found her. I want you to know that. Thirty-five years I knew her and I never saw her look more at peace.'

Smiling up at him, she took his hand and tugged, urging him to come down to her level.

'If I had been blessed with the son I always wanted...' She

squeezed his hand. 'You have no idea how proud you made your mother. No idea.'

Pavel smiled.

'I know,' he said, at a loss for any other words.

'Always working, always travelling, always on the move. It was all I could do to stop her talking about you for just one minute.'

They laughed together and, eventually, Pavel's laugh turned to tears. Mrs Vanová saw them as his faith in the things she had said.

Martina came in from the kitchen keeping her eyes on the tray of tea and biscuits she was carrying. As she placed it on the small coffee table in the middle of the room she noticed the puffy redness of her brother's eyes.

'I wondered how long that would take,' she said.

'I don't know, I think it's nice to see a man cry,' said Mrs Vanová. 'At least that way you know they've been listening.'

Martina put the tray down on the table.

'We'd both like to thank you for everything you've done,' said Pavel. 'I'm sorry you were on your own when you found her. It can't have been easy.'

'Don't be silly,' protested Mrs Vanová. 'You don't worry about things like that at my age. We always said one of us would find the other. I just never thought it would be me.'

'There's years left in you,' Martina said, handing her a cup of tea.

'I hope not,' replied Mrs Vanová. 'I can't imagine what this place will be like without your mother. I only wish we could have gone together.'

Pavel and Martina glanced at one another.

'Will you be alright on your own?' asked Pavel.

'I'm not on my own,' she replied. 'Don't forget I have my Milan. He's not much use, but then he wasn't much use when I married him, but I'm not on my own.'

Pavel and Martina both took a seat and each took a sip of their tea.

'Help yourself to a biscuit,' said Martina.

Pavel couldn't remember when he had last cried. As hard as he tried he couldn't recall when he had last lost his prized self-control. Not since I was a child, he thought to himself. Unsure if that counted, he reached out for a biscuit. Martina pushed the plate across the table into Pavel's reach and watched as he filled his hand with one of each variety. She was happy to see him again after all this time, no matter the circumstance. She had heard more about her brother than seen of him in the last few years. Whatever his work was, she had always been sure he used it as an excuse for his persistent absences more than anyone could reasonably expect to. She had never really understood what he did but that didn't seem to matter now. He had laid aside the uniform of his working life. He was her brother and nothing else.

Mrs Vanová held her cup on her lap and stared at the reflection on the surface of her tea. All she could hear was the sound of her futile knocks on her friend's door, echoing through the rooms of an empty house. She could only picture herself waiting hand and foot on a husband she had never understood, and had, despite years of patiently waiting, never come to love. He had, if nothing else, she consoled herself, lost the will to bully her. What mostly concerened Milan from day-to-day was waiting for the grave. Perhaps now she would be resigned to join him.

'I insist,' she said, 'the two of you eat with us tonight. So,' she added in Pavel's direction, 'don't go filling your bellies.'

'We can't expect you to cook for us,' said Martina. 'If anything you and Milan should be *our* guests, after all you've done.'

Pavel looked at her in alarm.

'That's very kind of you,' Mrs Vanová replied, 'but I'm sure a break from the house would do you both good. Anyhow, Milan never leaves the house these days and I couldn't come without him.'

'It seems like too much work for you,' Martina protested one last time.

'Nonsense,' she said, 'we have the grandchildren with us. I have all the help I need.'

Martina didn't have the energy for an argument she could tell she wouldn't win.

'Well, thank you, then.'

Pavel smiled, careful not to talk with his mouth full. He would settle for anything if it saved him from playing host.

Dinner at their neighbour's house sounded harmless by comparison.

'In that case I'd better get back,' said Mrs Vanová.

She tried to insist that they both remained seated but Martina showed her to the door. As Pavel eyed the biscuits he listened to them in the hallway arrange a time of six o'clock for dinner. He only had three hours to wait and he knew the more he ate that evening the more it would warm the old lady's heart. Somehow, Mrs Vanová had come to the opinion that men just never stopped growing. In the case of her husband this was true but Pavel would need to leave some room. He took an old paper and covered the plate. The front door closed and Martina appeared at the threshold of the living room.

'I'm glad you're here, you know,' she said.

Mrs Vanová's frankness appeared to have worn off on her.

'The night before you got here I hardly slept at all.'

'They couldn't get hold of me. I got here as soon as I could,' said Pavel.

'I didn't mean it like that. I just meant to say that I'm glad you're here.'

'That chest you were looking through,' he said, remembering what he'd been doing before their visitor had arrived. 'The one where you found that photo.'

'What about it?'

'Have you ever seen it before?'

Martina sat back in her chair to think the question over.

'Now you mention it, no, I haven't. The chest looks familiar but nothing inside it does.' She shook her head. 'Just some of Dad's old things I suppose.'

'You didn't see the envelopes?' asked Pavel.

'I don't remember.'

'There's a bunch of letters in a shoebox. They're all addressed to Dad but they've only got his name on, nothing else. How did they get there?'

'I don't know. What do they say?'

'They're all sealed. He hasn't opened a single one.'

He waited but she offered no response. He tried to gauge some reaction from her eyes.

'Well,' she said, eventually, 'I hope you're not suggesting that we open them.'

'Why not?'

'Because they're not ours to open. Simple as that.'

'Then who do they belong to? Tell me that. They don't belong to him any more.'

'Says who?'

'He's been dead for thirty years.'

Martina looked away. She didn't need to be reminded of family history, especially not by him.

'This house is ours now and everything in it,' he said. 'I don't want any secrets.'

'I wouldn't count on keeping this house if I were you. They'll get their hands on it one way or another.'

Pavel got up from his seat and knelt in front of Martina. He took her hand and softened his voice.

'I promise you,' he said, 'no one will ever come through that door unless you or I say so.'

'You don't know that,' she said.

'I promise,' he replied.

He knew it would take more than a promise. Her trust was weary from a lifetime of idle promises. Any day now, as soon as their mother's death had been formally registered, strangers would come to take what wasn't theirs to take, and the roots of her life would be severed. That was the truth as she saw it.

She took back the hand which he still held and pulled herself up from the chair.

'Those letters aren't ours to open,' she said. 'Let us keep some things sacred.'

XXIII

They walked to Mrs Vanová's house at a slow and calming pace, following the track marked out over time on the pine needle floor of the forest. The sun was low in the sky and it shone great shafts of light between the trunks of the trees. Birds could be heard but not seen, and the air was still and warm.

Their earlier conversation hadn't been forgotten but neither of them cared to mention it now. Instead, Pavel listened attentively while Martina ran through the names of the grandchildren she thought might be there to greet them.

After the chaos they'd anticipated of a houseful of children running wild, the silence of their neighbour's house struck them as more unsuitable than peaceful. From the gate at the end of the garden they could see the bright coloured tops of children's toys discarded in the long grass. The shutters on the windows were locked, and the wooden beams of the porch looked thirsty for paint.

'Hello,' Mrs Vanová called out, stepping out of the front door.

'We were expecting a welcoming party,' said Martina. 'Have we come to the wrong house?'

'Enjoy the peace and quiet while you can,' Mrs Vanová said. 'They've gone down to the lake, for the summer cinema, but they'll be back. They know you're coming.' She turned to Pavel. 'Tomaš is very excited.'

'Why? What have you been telling him?'

He had some idea of the tall stories that circulated the village, mostly due to his mother's boasting.

'Oh nothing. It's just his age. It's the way he is,' she explained, holding open the front door for them as they climbed the porch steps. 'He hasn't been to the city, so, anyone coming from the city and he can't stop asking questions.'

Mrs Vanová led them into the house.

'You remember Milan,' she said.

Pavel crossed the room to shake his hand. Milan didn't get up from his chair. Guests had nothing to do with him as far as he was concerned. The discourtesy, he thought, was his little secret.

Pavel could hardly recognise the old man. His hair was thin and white, his skin, pale and loose.

'Of course. It's nice to see you again,' said Pavel.

They shook hands. Milan folded his newspaper and put it to one side.

'Well,' said Martina, 'if all the children are out, you must need some help in the kitchen.'

'You can help me get some drinks,' replied Mrs Vanová.

The ladies went through to the kitchen, Pavel took off his jumper.

'It's warm outside. It's a wonderful evening. I forget how beautiful this part of the country is. Peaceful too.'

'I don't get out these days,' said Milan. 'The circulation in my legs gets worse and worse. I think soon the doctors will take them off.'

'I'm sorry to hear that,' said Pavel.

'They're no use to me.'

Pavel slowly folded his jumper and placed it neatly on the arm of a chair, taking all the time he could.

Mrs Vanová rushed to serve the drinks before Milan's lack of social graces became too obvious. Martina only succeeded in getting under her feet, bearing witness to her efforts rather than lessening them.

'They're nice and cold,' Mrs Vanová said, coming through with a tray laden with bottles of beer and glasses. She poured them one glass each and handed them out.

'If everyone's hungry then we can eat if you'd like.'

'Whatever you like,' said Martina.

'I can always eat,' Pavel said, keen to move things along.

Mrs Vanová took the necessary cutlery from her dresser draw and set the table.

'It's a beautiful view,' Pavel said, standing at the window.

'Sit down, sit down,' she said. 'I'll bring it through.'

One thing Pavel did miss, being away from home so often, was good Czech food. He knew that Russian cuisine, the usual substitute, was seen as a close relative and the differences were subtle, but then so, he liked to think, was his palate.

The reputation Mrs Vanová had attained as a cook had been built, above all, on her servings of svíčková na smetaně, a fillet of pork drowned in rich creamy sauce and a dollop of cranberry, served with the usual mountain of dumplings. This occasion was no different. She brought through a steaming hot dish, placed it in the middle of the table and urged her guests to help themselves while she prepared a plate for Milan.

When they were all seated, Milan poured what was left of his beer into his glass and cleared his throat.

'Well,' he said, 'I was very sorry to hear about your mother. She'll be sorely missed.' He raised his glass and, once the others had done so too, he took a respectful sip of his drink.

It was the first time he had spoken of her death in the company of his wife. She was touched and told herself that, as much as his toast was a mark of respect to the deceased, it was also his recognition of her loss. It was from such biased and generous interpretations that she could extract just enough kindness to persevere with the care and company of her husband. In the early years of their marriage she had needed them in daily doses, but since the opportunities had grown fewer, she had learned to make them last.

The four of them focused on their food and began to eat.

Pavel looked up to the others and smiled with his first mouthful. The sauce was rich and thick, the pork surprisingly tender.

Mrs Vanová smiled back modestly.

'So,' she said, while the others ate, 'do you have a day in mind for the funeral?'

'Saturday's best, I think,' replied Martina. She looked to her brother who nodded and chewed. 'It will be something very simple. There is no family that will come.'

'All the family are here already, that's why,' said Pavel.

'Yes,' said Martina. 'Something very simple.'

'Well if you need any help you know where to find me,' said Mrs Vanová.

'And where will you lay her to rest?' asked Milan.

'In the garden, I thought,' replied Martina. 'Next to Dad.'

Pavel nodded his approval while he chewed.

'Are you sure that's wise?' asked Milan.

A heavy silence descended on the table. Pavel was still chewing but began to speed up.

'Of course,' he said, as soon as he'd swallowed his food. 'But even if we weren't sure, that is where she belongs. Wouldn't you agree?'

'There is no doubt in my mind, none whatsoever,' replied Milan. 'In death they should be reunited. But I don't make the rules.'

'What do you mean?' asked Martina.

'I'm just saying, you can't be sure it's the best place to put her. You might think that they don't care what goes on out here but you're wrong.' His voice steadily rose as he made his point. 'They are everywhere.'

'What does this have to do with anything?' asked Pavel.

'You have to co-operate. It makes less trouble for everyone.'

'You're paranoid,' said Pavel.

'Yes, and that's why I'm still here.'

'No one cares about this stuff anymore.'

'You're wrong. But that's exactly what they want you to think.'

'That's enough,' exclaimed Mrs Vanová.

Martina put her head in her hands and began to cry. Mrs Vanová went to Martina, took her in her arms and scowled at her husband.

'It's always a conspiracy with you,' she snapped, 'never any sense.'

'We've already spoken about this,' Pavel said calmly to Milan. 'What you have to understand is that their time here is coming to an end. I've promised Martina we will keep the house, and we will.'

'Nonsense,' replied Milan. 'The Russians will never leave. Not in my lifetime.'

'No,' said Pavel, 'probably not in your lifetime. But they will soon be gone.'

'Maybe you should take Martina home,' said Mrs Vanová. 'I think she's had enough.'

Milan stayed at the table, breathing heavily and looking dejected while the others gathered at the door.

'I'm sorry,' Pavel said. 'I don't know why...'

'Don't you apologise, Pavel,' Mrs Vanová interrupted. 'I won't hear it. He deserves what he got and a lot more. I should know.'

Mrs Vanová opened the door for them and followed them out onto the porch.

'If anyone should be sorry it should be me,' Mrs Vanová said. Martina kissed her on the cheek.

'Come and see us tomorrow,' she said.

'I will.'

Martina turned to Pavel. She took his arm and pulled it around her shoulders like a scarf.

'Can we go?' she asked.

He decided that on the way home he wouldn't speak unless Martina spoke first. They took the path through the woods. It was twilight. The sun seemed to illuminate the sky but nothing else. Beyond the trees Pavel could hear cries of laughter as the grandchildren made their way home from the lake. It had been a good while, he thought, since he had heard laughter like that.

XXIV

The weather next morning was again in the vein of a summer that refused to leave. A cool breeze occasionally blew across the garden down to the shaded corner beneath the willow tree, where it would meet the sweat on Pavel's skin, and bring a welcome and refreshing chill. He had been working without a break for over two hours when he heard Martina's voice. She had called only his name, but as he approached the house he could detect the smell of breakfast in the air. He hadn't realised how hungry he was until then.

He had been digging in the corner of the garden since he got out of bed. An idea had struck him in the early hours and, unable to shake it from his head, he had gone to find his shovel and put it into practice.

He had begun by pouring a border of salt around the perimeter of where he wanted to dig. Then, he drove his shovel into the ground along his markings before cutting and rolling the turf away in one piece. Finally, with the earth exposed, he was able to dig. He dug very quickly to begin with but soon found a rhythm he knew he could sustain. Working every muscle in his body and feeling as awake as he ever had, he found a little peace of mind. Every drop he sweated was a tear he could not cry.

'Where have you been?' asked Martina. 'For a swim?'

'I've been working,' he replied. 'In the garden.'

'Doing what exactly?'

'I'll show you later,' he said, 'when I've finished.'

'Yuck!' she squealed as he brushed past her in the doorway, leaving a snail's trail of sweat across her bare arm.

Pavel sat down and ate his breakfast as though he hadn't eaten for a week. He listened while Martina recounted her dream of the night before. She had dreamt of their mother but didn't seem troubled. If anything, he thought, she seemed brighter than he'd dared hope she would, after the night before.

In her dream, she told him, she'd been sitting crossed-legged on the patio beneath the kitchen window. Their mother had talked to her through the open window, just as she had when they were both children. She couldn't remember any of the things their mother had said. Nevertheless, she explained, she felt better for having been in her company.

After breakfast Pavel returned to the corner of the garden. As the day wore on the temperature rose but he worked as hard as ever. He could smell that Martina was baking in the kitchen. The sun shone very brightly but it couldn't break through the thick canopy of shade provided by the willow. Even in the leafless days of winter, when the sun paid an unexpected visit, and the sky appeared bluer than ever, the ground beneath the willow tree remained untouched, sheltered by a woven parasol of branches.

This was the corner his mother had chosen for his father's final resting place. Now, he thought, they are in some way reunited. A just reward for his mother's devotion in all her years of solitude. A thank you to his father, he liked to think, for all the years his spirit had guided her harmlessly towards the end. Standing chest-deep in the grave he had spent all day digging for his mother, as near to his father's as he could go, Pavel felt that things were being done as they should be.

The wind began to blow stronger than before. He could not only hear it beneath the willow but also in the woods beyond the garden. He stood his shovel in the earth and slowly straightened his back. He closed his eyes and imagined the wind blowing through his head, each gust taking another worry with it. Things will be better than this, he thought, but they will never be the same.

'Pavel,' he heard Martina call.

He climbed out of the grave and called back.

'Yes.'

'We have a visitor,' she said, watching him walk up the gentle slope of the garden. Next to her stood Mrs Vanová holding a large plate covered in tin foil. As he reached them, Martina took the plate and turned to go into the house.

'I'll make some tea,' she said. 'Take a seat and I'll bring it out.'

There was a garden table and chairs on the patio by the kitchen window. As usual the chairs had been tilted forward to lean against the table so that any rain that fell during the night wouldn't settle and rot the wood. There had been no rain since Pavel had arrived but he carried out the chore every night regardless. If his mother was somewhere watching him, he wanted to be sure of her approval.

'I thought I'd bring you some food for Saturday but it smells like someone's been cooking all morning,' Mrs Vanová said, as he righted the chairs.

'I know. You'd think it was a wedding,' he said, and offered her a seat.

'How many people are you expecting?'

'Not too many, I hope.'

Noticing that the kitchen window was open he resorted to a whisper. 'She's just trying to keep herself busy, that's all.'

'And you too I see,' Mrs Vanová said, eyeing the sweat that covered him.

'Well, there's a lot to be done,' he said. 'I hadn't given it much thought until last night.'

'That's why I came.'

'You've done more than enough already,' he said. 'We'll manage.'

'No, I didn't mean that. I meant about Milan, and the way he behaved last night.'

Watching the tray and where she was stepping with equal care Martina appeared with the tea. She placed the tray on the table and checked her chair for damp.

'So, what's the topic of the day?' she asked, sitting down and reaching for the teacups.

'I was just about to apologise for last night,' said Mrs Vanová. 'I don't know what goes through that man's head sometimes. I wanted to say I was sorry.'

'There's no reason for you to feel sorry,' said Pavel. 'It's quite understandable. It's the way people are. It's the way they've made them. I should have known better than to say what I said.'

'It did him good. He's always been a bully. You shouldn't feel sorry for him.'

'It's not easy for any of us,' he added, 'but holding grudges won't make things easier.'

Mrs Vanová shook her head and took a sip of tea. 'If your mother could see you now,' she said, looking at each of them in turn.

'Come on then,' said Pavel, getting up from the table and setting off for the corner of the garden. 'I'll show you what I've been doing all morning.'

They followed close behind while Pavel led the way. As they approached the corner where her father was buried, Martina began to shorten her steps. She stopped a few feet short of where the others had walked.

Pavel gazed down into the unfinished grave.

'It's like I was saying last night,' he said, 'this is where she belongs. Nothing can change that.'

'Is it deep enough?' asked Mrs Vanová.

She had always leaned towards cremation herself. The smooth cold walls of mud and the small brown puddles of water, formed in the footprints where Pavel had stood, did nothing to change her mind.

'It's not finished yet,' said Pavel, 'but it will be by tonight.'

He looked over to Martina. She was still standing in the sunlight, staring at the hole he'd dug. The sun was making her squint and he couldn't judge her reaction. He walked back, put his arm around her and guided her slowly toward the edge of the grave.

'On Saturday we can bury her here. They'll be together again. We can put flowers on Dad's grave. A congratulations.'

'For what?' she asked, with tears in her voice.

'He's got his wife back. Don't you think he's happy?'

'I know you don't think it is,' she said, slowly, 'but what if all this is for nothing? Wouldn't it be better to put her somewhere public? Just in case?'

Pavel bent down, placed his hands on the edge of the grave and jumped down. There was the soft squelch of mud beneath his feet as he stepped towards his shovel.

'I'm tired of promising you, so you'll just have to wait and see,' he said. 'There's no need for just-in-cases.'

He pulled the shovel from its sheath of mud and began to dig again, as he had all morning, rhythmically inflicting wounds into the earth.

Mrs Vanová watched Pavel burrow his way into the ground, turning over large chunks of earth and making a show of his strength. She detected something strange in the way he spoke, some insistence he didn't want questioned. She didn't think they were wild predictions he was making, born out of blind fury or denial.

'This is the country, Pavel, try to remember that,' she said. 'Maybe we're not up to speed on things.'

On his next lunge Pavel left his shovel in the earth and turned to listen.

'What do you mean?'

'I'm not going to be your judge, but if there were some way you knew for certain the house is safe maybe you should tell your sister.'

'If I could tell you that...' Pavel sighed and leaned back against the shovel.

'Tell me what?' Martina asked.

'I've already told you. The house is ours.'

He felt trapped, as though the grave in which he stood was his own. He was being buried alive with questions he couldn't answer.

'Very well. That's good enough,' said Mrs Vanová. All she had wanted was to seek reassurance for Martina's sake. Now it had turned into a confrontation and she felt responsible.

'How can you be so sure?' Martina cried.

She clenched her fists and began to tremble. Pavel scrambled out of the grave. Taking his sister by the arms, he squeezed hard to stop her from shaking and spoke gently into her ear.

'Because it's arranged, because it's arranged,' he said, repeating the words over and over again. 'I've seen to it because I can.'

Her heart felt close to stopping. She almost wished it would.

XXV

It was only ever a few minutes after the sun had risen that Martina followed suit. She hadn't slept well all night and, now that she had woken, she knew she wouldn't sleep again.

She had spent most of the previous evening alone in the house, making a list of things to be done the following day. She'd also gone through every drawer in the house looking for her mother's old recipes but had had no luck. Every drawer she had opened contained something that triggered her memory. It wasn't long before she forgot the recipes and began looking for the sake of looking. Pavel's digging had kept him outside as long as the daylight had lasted. It had been no effort to avoid him. When he finally came into the house he went straight to bed. They both knew a reconciliation was more likely to be achieved in the morning.

Down in the kitchen she made herself coffee and cut a thick slice of bread to smother in butter and jam before she consulted her list.

Pavel had taken it on himself to make most of the practical arrangements for Saturday. This suited Martina as it gave her more time to get the house in order and the food prepared. She wasn't sure how many mouths she should be expecting to feed but she didn't want to be caught short or have people going hungry. More to the point, in her eyes, people might start to think that she wasn't coping. She wanted to keep herself busy and if this was all the sleep she could count on getting, at least the cooking could fill up her days.

The first job on her list was a trip to the shops to stock up. She knew it didn't make the best sense to go shopping before she had found her mother's recipes but she was confident she could remember most of the ingredients. It was measurements and timing she would need them for most.

She went out to the woodshed that stood in the front garden. It was dark inside, and hard to tell one rusting piece of metal from another. Once her eyes were more accustomed to the dark she wheeled her mother's old bike out into the garden. The bike was older than she was and it was showing its age. The spokes were loose and a few were missing altogether. Paint was peeling from the frame and the chain looked rusty and brittle. There was a wooden trailer with two wheels attached to the back with hooks beneath the saddle. She could vividly remember the day her father made it, so their mother no longer had to shop in dribs and drabs or be dependant on how strong he was feeling.

As children, they'd only ever had one use for it. Pavel rode the bike along the trails in the woods while she sat in the trailer behind, holding on for her life and screaming at the top of her voice. It was a daily routine in the summer while the tracks were dry. One day Pavel decided, as they approached a steep incline, deep in the woods, to jump clear of the bike. Martina had frozen. By the time she had decided it would be better to jump, the bike and trailer had jack-knifed and thrown her clear. Her fall had been bad. She took the brunt of the landing on her chest which took the air clean out of her lungs. When the bike came down it landed on top of her, the teeth of the cogs catching her in the face.

Pavel pleaded with her not to tell their parents, but with one less tooth than she had set out with, and blood on her dress, it was a promise she could hardly keep. She had to tell the story every time someone enquired about the scar that followed the underside of her jaw line.

The bike had been banned and locked in the shed where it had stayed until now. As she had no intention to venture into the woods she presumed the ban could be lifted.

'Can I offer you a lift?' Pavel asked, putting his shoes on at the door.

'I think you know the answer to that,' she replied, stroking the line of her scar.

'At least let me have a look at it,' said Pavel.

He walked over to the shed and began to look for some oil.

'Only if you're quick. I've got lots to do.'

He pumped some air into the tyres and oiled the chain.

'Have you finished what you were doing?' she asked.

She was looking toward the shaded corner of the garden.

'I finished it last night,' he replied. 'That's why I went straight to bed.'

'And how are your arms?'

'Stiff, very stiff,' he said, giving them a stretch just to make sure.

'You should have soaked them in the bath before you went to bed. I'm surprised they still work.'

'I'd have fallen asleep in the bath,' he said.

'Well, at least you wouldn't smell the way you do.'

Pulling on the brakes Pavel rocked the bike back and forth. When he was satisfied, he patted the saddle.

'So, what are you doing today?' she asked, climbing onto the bike. He walked up to the top of the garden and held open the gate for her.

'I'll have some breakfast then go back up to the loft. Finish off what we started.'

'Just have coffee for now,' she said. 'I'll make your breakfast when I'm back. I won't be long. And don't throw anything out until I've seen it.' She began pushing down on the pedals and building up speed. 'And keep an eye out for Mum's old recipes. I can't find them anywhere so they must be up there.'

'Anything else?' he asked, as she delicately steered the bike through the gate.

'Go and have a bath.'

She lifted herself out of the saddle, peddling as hard as she could. Pavel watched her disappear down the track and hoped that the brakes would hold out.

Back inside the house he made himself some coffee. He remembered that the light bulb had begun to flicker, so, he took a torch from the dresser draw and climbed the ladder back to the loft. He stepped over the unfinished boxes and sat down next to the chest.

More than anything he wanted to know who the letters were from. He took a letter and held it up to the light but that only made it silhouette. He turned the torch on and shone the beam into the back of the envelope. He was desperate to catch a glimpse of a name or town, anything that might satisfy his curiosity, but the envelope was too thick to let through enough light. He flicked through the envelopes counting and checking that his father's name had been written on all of them. It had, and unless he came across any more, there were thirty-three letters in all. He packed up the chest and carried it over to a chair by the window. Excited at the prospect of meeting his father again after all these years, he began rummaging into the old man's past.

Martina was right. If he ever wanted to remember how his father had looked, he need only look in the mirror. From the very first page of the photo album, in pictures of his father as a young man, Pavel saw himself over and over again. It was strange looking into a world that knew nothing of him, times when he hadn't existed, but there they were in black and white. His father's features passed down by his father before him. He wondered if he would continue the line.

With that thought still hanging in his mind, he closed the album along with his eyes. It was incredibly peaceful in the roof of the house. I'm tired from all that digging, he thought, and slowly succumbed to an irresistible sleep.

XXVI

Martina decided to push the bike through the village. There was little traffic but she nevertheless felt that her cargo of food was too precious to risk. The village was quiet with few faces around but those that were seemed familiar. She was struck by the meandering way the people went about their business. Brno, the city where she now lived, had offered her the anonymity she craved when she first left home. She didn't miss it now it was gone. Perhaps, if Pavel was true to his word, and the house was theirs to keep, she might never go back.

Some people crossed the road to offer their sympathies. Some crossed the road to avoid her which she didn't find upsetting. The moments of condolence were more embarrassing and she was glad to be spared them once or twice.

Once the shopping was done and she had rested in the square for a while, she decided to head home and make Pavel some breakfast. There used to be benefits to living out of town - the freedom to roam and wreak havoc in the woods was one. Now, however, with a heavy load in the trailer and a steep hill ahead of her, she thought the benefits were more suited to those with young legs.

When she arrived home, she left the bike and the shopping in the shadow of the house, and went inside.

'Pavel,' she called out.

Her legs felt like jelly. He would have to bring the shopping in before the sun turned the food into wasted money.

She continued to call for Pavel as she walked unsteadily up the stairs to the loft, but got no answer. By the time she reached the top of the ladder she'd guessed he'd be asleep. She found him tucked away in the corner slumped in the old chair from his bedroom.

'Well,' she said, loud enough to wake him, 'what a hard morning you must have had.'

'I was resting my eyes,' he replied.

'Well, I need to rest my legs, so, if you bring the shopping in, then I might believe you.'

He rose stiffly from the awkward position he'd slept in. Anticipating the size of her shopping spree he shook out his arms to loosen them.

'Whatever you say.'

Pavel took the bags through to the kitchen and began putting the shopping into the cupboards, as best as he could remember where things went. Just as he was starting on the last bag, he heard Martina bounding down the stairs.

'I've found them,' she cried, busting into the kitchen and waving a bunch of papers in the air.

'Found what?' Pavel asked, laughing at her.

'Mum's recipes, they're all here.'

She began to lay them out in front of her on the kitchen table. The thought of bringing her mother's creations to life gave Martina overwhelming comfort. She went to the kitchen dresser and from the bottom drawer she took the apron she had last seen her mother wearing. She put it on and went back to the recipes.

Pavel stood at her shoulder watching as she turned the pages, running her finger along the lines of fading ink.

'Makes you hungry just looking, doesn't it,' she said.

He didn't reply. He was staring at the recipes. He gripped Martina's arm to get her attention.

'What is it?'

'The letters,' he said, pointing at the table.

'They're recipes, not letters.'

He let go of her arm and hurried out of the kitchen.

'What is it?' she called after him.

She could hear him running through the house and then on the stairs to the loft. He came back into the kitchen holding the old envelopes and laid them on top of the recipes.

'They're from Mum,' he said.

Martina compared the handwriting. The inks were of different colour and the writing in the recipes less neat and deliberate, but it was obvious the same hand had written them both.

She looked up and saw the excitement on Pavel's face.

'This doesn't mean that she wrote whatever's inside, and it certainly doesn't mean that we're opening them.'

'Are you mad?' he was barely able to control his voice. 'There are over thirty letters in that chest. Are you trying to tell me that Mum took all his old letters and just sealed them up with his name on them?'

'Then why haven't they been opened?'

'Because he never read them,' he shouted. 'Why do you think?'

His patience had run dry. Reacting first, Pavel grabbed an envelope from the table and began to rip it open. She lunged at him and desperately tried to snatch it back. He held the letter too high for her to reach. She turned her back on him and brought her hands up to her face. She didn't make a sound.

'I'm sorry,' he said quietly.

He handed her the letter. It was torn and crumpled but still unread. She tucked it into her apron pocket.

'There are some things I need from the shops,' Martina said, wiping her nose as she consulted the recipes. 'Will you go for me?'

He walked to the door and fetched his shoes.

In the kitchen Martina made him a short shopping list. He knew that most things on the list would probably be somewhere in one of the cupboards, but he said nothing. She handed it to him and he pushed it into his pocket.

He saw the bike in the garden but left it there. He felt like walking. He took the route through the woods that would bring him out closest to the village.

It didn't take him long to buy everything on the list. He added on two bottles of beer for himself and, when he was finished, he took a seat on a bench near to the bus station and watched the people who had gathered for the next service to Prague. He opened his beer and drank it while it was cold.

XXVII

'Why don't you just let him read them?' Mrs Vanová asked. 'He doesn't have to tell you what they say.'

She had come to offer her services in getting the house ready for Saturday. Martina had thanked her but refused the offer, before telling her about the letters.

'It's not that,' Martina said, trying to explain the situation to her guest as much as to herself. 'I don't care what they say. I just think they're personal. They're not ours to open.'

'Then whose are they? She can't take them with her.'

'That's what I had in mind,' replied Martina. 'We could bury them with her.' She looked for a smile or nod of agreement.

'I don't think that's a good idea.'

Martina sighed.

'Whatever the letters say they have served their purpose,' she went on. 'If your mother wrote them, their job was done as soon as the ink was dry.'

'I suppose,' said Martina.

'She loved your father very much. You don't have to fear what those letters say. Don't bury your feelings with them. You'll be wasting a beautiful opportunity if you let them go, and you'll never stop thinking about them.' Martina slowly nodded. 'So, where are they?' asked Mrs Vanová.

'I have one here,' she said, taking the envelope from her apron pocket and holding it against her lips. She stared at Mrs Vanová as though waiting for instructions, then winced and turned as she heard Pavel tussling with his shoes at the back door.

'Good morning, Mrs Vanová,' Pavel said, as he entered. He could tell that his sister had been crying again. By now he could feel it in the air.

'Good morning, Pavel,' replied Mrs Vanová. The two of them looked at Martina but her back was turned. 'I'll have to leave you I'm afraid. Milan will need his lunch soon and I don't dare let him make it himself. He'd burn the house down.'

'Thank you,' Martina said, turning to face her.

The metal latch on the door clicked as Mrs Vanová let herself out. Once they were alone, Martina placed the letter on the table.

'I'd like to read the letters.'

Pavel leaned against the sink, unsure how to react.

'Don't ask me why,' she said, raising a hand to deflect any questions. He said nothing.

'I'm having some wine. Do you want some?' Martina asked, on her way out of the kitchen.

'Whatever you're having,' he replied, still surprised by her change of heart.

He watched through the kitchen window as she walked barefoot to the garden cellar. Unable to wait any longer, he gathered up the rest of the letters. He met her at the front door with a corkscrew and two glasses. He handed her the letters and took the bottle from her. She walked through to the living room and sat in the sunken chair by the fire. He took the wine into the kitchen and poured two large glasses.

'Don't start without me,' he called to her.

Martina flicked through the pile, looking for some kind of chronological order. There wasn't any that could be told from the envelopes alone. Pavel came through and handed her a glass. She took a sip of wine and glanced up at Pavel whose impatience was obvious. She tore open the envelope, pulled the letter out and unfolded it.

'They're dated,' she said, 'we should get them in order.'

They put down their wine, opened the rest of the envelopes and laid the letters out flat on the floor so they could check the dates. Pavel found it hard to stop his eyes straying any further down the pages. Unconnected words leaped out at him, increasing his anticipation. Martina had more discipline and rapidly shuffled the letters into order. When she was done she returned to her seat and took a gulp of wine.

'You know I'm not doing this just because of you, don't you?' she asked.

'Nobody's forcing you.'

She straightened out the first letter onto her lap. He closed his eyes and listened as she began to read.

Dear Dominik,   *16th November, 1968*

I don't even know if I should address this letter to you or not. I think I'm writing to myself as much as to you.

I'm starting to think that you won't be coming home for a long time. Hiding in my head somewhere there is a voice. I hear it mostly when I dream. It tells me that things would be easier if I thought of you as dead. In the daytime I struggle to keep this voice quiet, then the children ask me when they can see you again. What can I say to them? That's when it seems hardest. But everything seems hard.

Pavel asks about you the most but I can see Martina is always thinking of you. She only asks about you when no one else is around. She knows that something is wrong but she never mentions it in front of Pavel. She's a big sister to him more than ever now. I won't talk about the children. I believe you will see them soon for yourself. I will try and listen to my heart instead of my head because it tells me you're coming home.

All my love

Jana

Pavel took a while to open his eyes. He tried to think logically. He was almost certain that his father had never read the letter, perhaps had never been intended to read it. Except for the date there was nothing that sounded concrete.

Martina wasn't sure whether she wanted to read on.

'What do you think it means?' Pavel asked, surprised to be the one voicing the questions. Martina sipped her wine. 'It's nice being mentioned though, isn't it,' he added.

'Yes,' she said. 'Do you want me to carry on?'

'Would you rather I read?' he asked.

'No, it's not that,' she said, reaching for the next letter from the pile. 'It's just that they seem... well, it seems a little strange, that's all.'

'Carry on,' he said, closing his eyes again. 'You sound just like Mum. It makes it all the more authentic.'

Dominik,   *6th January 1969*

I'm not sure if this is going to help or not but the last letter did and I need some help. Christmas was harder than anything else.

There's been barely any news from the city and none about you, which is all I care about. Pavel asks more and more questions but Martina hardly speaks. She knows, and she knows that I've been lying all this time. I am coming to the end of all hope.

I have written letters to everyone I could think of. I have to know what has happened to you. Sometimes I imagine, I even hope that you are in a prison somewhere. I pray that those bastards have taken you from me and that one day God will return you. That is the best I dare pray for. I'm fearing and expecting the worst. Are you dead? If you are then why don't you tell me?

I love you and the children love you,

Jana

'That doesn't make any sense,' Pavel said, sitting up. 'Why, if she was writing to him, would she ask him if he was dead? What's she talking about?'

He jabbed his finger at the letter to emphasise his point.

'These letters aren't addressed to him, can't you see that? I don't think we should read anymore.'

'No way,' protested Pavel immediately. 'I can't leave it like this. We have to know what she's talking about.'

'I don't,' Martina said, sure that she already knew.

'Well, I do.'

He went over to her chair and held out his hand. 'I'll read them myself.'

'Can't you see what you've already been told? How can you think you were ever meant to read them?'

'It's too late now.'

There was no way of saving him from the truth, she thought. She picked up another letter and he took his seat again. She brushed a stray hair from her face and hooked it behind her ear. She slowly began to read.

Dominik,   *6th March 1969*

I'd like to think that it's over now, and all doubt is at an end. With all my heart I hope that I have done the best thing for the children. In some ways they may now grow stronger, that's my only comfort.

I buried you yesterday but there has still been no news. I don't know what became of you, I think now that I never will. I know in my heart that you've gone, otherwise I couldn't have put the children through all of this. You wouldn't have left me like this.

It is the strangest peace that I find sometimes in the still of a room when I am all alone. I know that it's you who visits. You bring a fragile peace to me in those moments, though you never stay long. It is then that I feel whole and I pray that these moments grow longer.

Perhaps I should feel guilt for all the deceiving I've done but I don't. All the guilt that I had inside me has been buried by my love for the children. They are my only concern. Everything else is beyond my understanding. I think Martina has known for some time that she wouldn't ever see you again. She hasn't been herself since Christmas and she's long since stopped her questions. Pavel continues to ask but hopefully all that will change. He's as active as ever, even more mischief without you here. He calls your name now whenever he cries and I find that hard to bear.

I hope you visit the children as you visit me and fill their hearts with love.

I will write again soon,

All my love

Jana

Martina sat with the letter hanging from her fingertips. The sedate rhythm of the old clock in the corner was all that she could hear. She had always pictured her mother with a loving smile. Somewhere in the course of the last letter the smile had gone. Now, she could only see the broken spirit of a woman not much older than herself.

She placed the letter back on the pile and got to her feet. All the feeling seemed to have deserted her legs as they gently shook under the weight of her body. She took her near-empty glass of wine through to the kitchen and tipped what was left into the sink.

She walked back to the living room and crouched down in front of the fireplace. She took the letters in her hand and held them tightly at one end while she struck a match on the stone of the mantelpiece. When the sparks had become a flame she slowly waved the match under the letters. She threw the letters onto the grate before the flames reached her fingers and watched as they curled up and burned.

She made her way down the garden towards the shaded corner and the willow tree. She could hear him long before she got there.

Pavel was black with soil, his hair matted and wet. He was slipping in the mud as he fumbled for his footing. When he found his balance he stabbed and drove the shovel deep into the wall of the grave, tunnelling through to his father's. Hope lay beneath that headstone, and so long as there was any of that, he would keep digging.

Martina turned her back on the grave and began walking back to the house. She couldn't bring herself to stay and watch. Either there was nothing there at all or he would discover an empty coffin.

XXVIII

MOSCOW 1988

In this weather nobody shaves as often as they normally would, thought Pavel, standing half-dressed at his window, stroking the growth of hair on his face. The snow fell so heavily he could barely make out the flats on the opposite side of his street. When a Moscow winter gets into its stride, he told himself, it makes good sense to nurture any defence from the cold that you can. He felt confident that his appearance would be seen as a symptom of the weather, and not his state of mind.

His flat was basic, the standard issue for an agent of his rank. It didn't take him long to pack. When he was done he gathered his things at the door. He put on his coat and gloves and left, making no last-minute checks. There was no contemplative moment at the door before he closed it for the last time. He treated his departure with the same cold indifference that he'd treated everything since the funeral. The overnight bag slung over his shoulder was all that he could take with him into his future. Happily, his past would have to be left behind.

It was early morning and the snow was falling at such a rate that footprints seemed to disappear as soon as they'd been left. He couldn't have wished for a better start to the day, he told himself. From the moment I step outside, he thought, until the day that I die, I will leave no trace on this earth.

Keeping away from the snow-covered kerb and close to

the buildings, Pavel walked to work. He found the innocuous-looking side door to the Lubyanka without thinking about where he was going, gazing down instead at the carpet of snow. He stamped his feet at the door, dislodging clumps of snow from his shoes before he pushed his way inside.

The usual stifling heat filled the stairwell. He hurried to remove his jacket before climbing the stairs. As calmly as he could, and awkwardly aware that everything had to seem as normal as always, he punched in the long code that opened the door and walked into the office.

'You're late!'

A young girl crept out from behind her desk, looking as though something had set her on edge.

Long familiar with her dramas, Pavel met this one with unconcern.

'No, Anna, I'm not,' he said, tapping his watch. He took a cigarette from the box on Anna's desk and lit it.

'Well, they've been waiting in there for twenty minutes, so what difference does it make?' she demanded to know.

'The difference is twenty minutes, which makes him early, whereas I am on the dot.'

He stubbed out the cigarette, content with a few brief drags. It was also a little early for him to be smoking. He stood in front of Anna and held his arms out to the side. Scanning his jacket for pieces of fluff she brushed him down as though he were about to meet her parents.

'Just in the nick of time, more like,' she said, fussing with his tie. 'Now go on in and don't upset him. Remember, I'm the one who has to put up with him for the rest of the day.'

Pavel's heart sank a little. He had grown fond of Anna and had come to depend on her little rituals. He wondered if she made such a fuss of all the other agents who passed through her office. He suspected not. She made him feel special. Anna turned away from him and knocked on Grechko's door.

Grechko had been sitting with his legs crossed, his chair pushed back from his desk, listening to the muffled conversation coming from the other side of the door. The snippets of Anna and Pavel's banter that floated through highlighted the silence that hung between him and the young Irishman sitting opposite him. Although he would never have admitted it, Grechko found the silence mildly embarrassing. The young Irishman, on the other hand, guessed the awkward atmosphere was one final test of his nerve.

He sat as still as he could, clutching to his lap a completely inadequate coat for the temperature outside, and yet he was sweating. He hoped Grechko would pass it off as traces of melting snow and listened intently to the progress being made next door.

Anna didn't wait for her knock to be answered. She knew Grechko grew irritable in the company of the Irish. 'In a world of their own,' he would declare after each of their infrequent visits. How they ever presumed to be taken seriously was beyond his understanding. When Anna pushed open the door, his eyes lit up as Pavel stepped into the room.

'Mr Barracurra,' Grechko announced by way of introduction. The young Irishman stood and shook Pavel's hand. 'Mr Barracurra, this is your courier. As promised, the finest we have.'

'Sean Barracurra, pleased to meet you,' said the Irishman.

'Likewise,' said Pavel.

Pavel helped himself to his second cigarette of the day from the wooden case on Grechko's desk. They were red Marlboro. It was never too early for luxury.

He lit his cigarette, striking a match and sucking at the flame in one continuous motion before sitting down. He took the ashtray from Grechko's desk and balanced it on his knee. He couldn't dare try to hold his hands still – he could tell they were shaking. They are the hands of a coward, he told himself, and hid one in his lap. With the other he continued smoking.

Sean leaned back into his chair fiddling with the coat that was back in his lap. His new colleague seemed more interested in his cigarette than making him feel welcome. He decided that he didn't trust him and wiped the sweat from the back of his neck.

Grechko took a set of keys from one of the drawers in his desk and threw them to Pavel.

'There's a car ready for you downstairs,' he said.

'Assuming you're ready to leave?'

Pavel nodded.

'Now, for the duration of your trip, Mr Barracurra, you will refer to your courier here as Mr King. When your travels are over, I don't imagine you'll be seeing him again. If for any reason you do, obviously, you are not to acknowledge your acquaintance, unless he does so first. Understood?'

'Mr King?' he asked. 'That doesn't sound very Russian.'

Grechko smiled at the belligerent tone of the question. The Irishman was clearly trying to assert himself. He didn't care about the name.

'Not that it's any of your concern,' said Grechko, 'but Mr King is not Russian, he's Czech.' Sean's face reddened. 'But, not to worry, we are all one big family these days.'

Stubbing his cigarette out, Pavel smiled in Sean's direction. Grechko stood up and walked around his desk.

'Mr Barracurra, have a safe trip. You are in safe hands. I hope that we've been of some use to your cause.' He shook Sean's hand, using up the last of his faked cordiality. 'Anna will help you with your coat. I have a little business with Mr King.'

Sean let himself out, relieved that at least one thing was over.

XXIX

Grechko's reputation had been well known to Pavel long before they had ever crossed paths. By the time he met him, years of Chinese whispers had taken their toll and Grechko had stood before him like a colossus. It was only now, standing on the outside looking in, that he could see past the reputation. It wasn't that Pavel held any personal grudge towards him; it was the colour of the flag he waved that so offended him. It's just that I've opened my eyes, he'd begun to tell himself, and they're the ones who opened them for me.

When Sean had left the room and shut the door behind him, Grechko perched himself on the edge of his desk. Pavel took another cigarette. This little meeting was unexpected. His hand shook less with Sean out of the room but he still felt the need for some distraction.

'You should know by now that I'm always honest with you,' began Grechko. Pavel nodded intently. In Grechko's company he rarely elaborated on answers when a simple yes or no would do. 'I can't say I've been asked any myself, but I get the feeling people are asking questions about you.'

'What sort of questions?' Pavel asked.

He felt he had no choice but to appear in the dark, even offended by the suggestion. Grechko took a deep breath.

'Are you happy with your work?' he asked. 'That's all I need to know.'

'I'm very happy with my work. Aren't you?'

'It isn't a question of standards, it's a question of worth.'

'Am I restless, you mean?'

Grechko shrugged his shoulders.

'You tell me,' he said.

'Maybe you're right,' said Pavel, twisting the line of questioning, 'maybe it's time for a new challenge, something different.' He stared down at the floor contemplatively.

'Maybe,' Grechko said, lifting himself off the desk, 'but don't think about it too much. You've had a difficult year, losing your mother. These things take time.'

Grechko returned to his seat behind the desk. He was never comfortable expressing concern to people, or feelings of any kind. Pavel placed the ashtray back on the desk and got to his feet. He took another cigarette for later.

'I'll expect to see you in six days then,' said Grechko, 'or a phone call as usual.'

'It's a reliable run,' said Pavel, 'I can't see what would go wrong.'

Pavel moved towards the door. With each step, the anticipation of closing a chapter in his life grew stronger. Things will no longer be scripted within the confines of these four walls, he said to himself. I'll never see your face again, he thought. He looked back but Grechko didn't look up from the papers on his desk. He left the office and closed the door behind him.

Sean was standing with his back to the window that overlooked the courtyard below. Anna was nowhere to be seen. As Pavel stepped into the office Sean turned and looked down into the courtyard.

'That our car?' he asked, pointing down. He had relaxed back into his own accent.

Pavel walked over to the window, checking for the keys in his pocket. He glanced down at the familiar black saloon and nodded.

'Let's go then,' Sean said, trying to put some authority into his voice. 'I want this thing over.'

While Sean made his way out of the room Pavel stayed at the window. It was clear to him that Sean didn't think the same level of respect was needed as with Grechko. He couldn't feel offended although he knew he was probably meant to. The opinions of a man whose thoughts would never mature into actions were simply inoffensive.

Outside the snow was still falling as heavily as before. Pavel hurried across the courtyard to the boot of the car and put his coat inside. Sean followed him but kept his coat on. Pavel let himself in, started the engine and began playing with the controls on the heater.

'Will ya let me in,' Sean shouted, knocking on the passenger window.

Pavel opened his door.

'Can you open gate?' he asked.

Looking over to the heavy wooden doors that led to the road, Sean could tell they wouldn't be going anywhere with them shut. He threw a bag onto his seat and slammed the door.

Pavel watched him scurry across the courtyard while he felt the air from the heater slowly turn warm on his legs.

'That's something else out there,' Sean said, once he was inside the car. He took a packet of cigarettes from his bag and put one between his lips, all the time shivering. He offered one to Pavel who only refused the offer after feeling around for the spare Marlboro from Grechko's desk in his pocket.

'I'll leave them up here,' Sean said, placing the packet on the dashboard, 'help yourself.'

No matter how badly I might crave, Pavel told himself, I must leave that packet untouched.

Trying not to spin the tyres on the snow, he put the car into gear and pulled away. He thought about asking Sean to close the gates once they had driven through but that seemed improper. Someone else would tend to them. He pulled out into the early-morning traffic, worked his way across to the furthest lane and headed towards the outskirts of the city.

Everything was restricted by the weather and the traffic,

though not congested, moved slowly. Sean turned to his window in search of a different view. Well-wrapped bodies shuffled through the snow or huddled together, waiting for the next tram.

'So, is that true what he said back there?' asked Sean. 'Are you the best one they've got? Or was that just for my benefit?'

'Don't worry,' Pavel replied, concentrating on the road. 'It's not difficult job, any one of us could do it.'

'So why pick you?'

'Everybody busy.'

'Have you smuggled guns before then?' asked Sean.

'Many times,' answered Pavel.

'All over the world, I suppose.'

Looking for something to discourage the conversation Pavel turned the radio on. A good reception was unlikely with the weather like it was but he tried anyway. The background noise of static and the occasional wave of clear reception were enough to keep Sean quiet. After a minute or two of searching Pavel found the only reasonably consistent signal. Two elderly-sounding men were in mid-discussion and there was no apparent likelihood of music, but their voices felt more comfortable than Sean's conversation.

'What are they talking about?' asked Sean.

'Philby,' replied Pavel.

'Who?'

'Kim Philby.'

'Who's she?' asked Sean.

'She is he.'

'Well, who is he?'

'He was spy. He defect here.'

Pavel glanced across to see if he had jogged Sean's memory. Seeing his face at a different angle it occurred to him that Sean was not as old as he had first guessed.

'Before many years,' he added, 'twenty years... more.'

'And they still talk about him?'

'He died before six months.'

'Before six months,' Sean repeated and laughed to himself.

He reached down into his bag and began to rummage through it.

'Well, I don't speak Russian,' he said, producing a tape from his bag, 'so could we have some music instead?'

Pavel's curiosity as to what music a citizen of the free world might carry in his bag was almost overwhelming but he managed to confine himself to a nonchalant shrug of the shoulders.

'The Rolling Stones,' Sean said, inserting the tape. 'Ever heard of them?'

Pavel shot him a glance, acknowledging the mocking tone of the question. He wouldn't answer him on principal now but he didn't know who they were.

The sound of drums erupted from the speakers and Sean began to tap his feet and slap his knees. He looked out of his window at the white coat that lay over everything in Moscow that morning. This is it, he thought, and a shiver ran through his body. Where there had been fear there was adrenaline now and what had been nerves was excitement.

Richards struck the opening chord and the stress that Sean had suppressed all morning abated as the rhythm gathered momentum. He closed his eyes and smiled. I'm more than a thousand miles from the rest of them, thought Sean, sitting next to the KGB. Things he had once called regrets, now seemed more like lessons he had learned. He felt more content with the here and now than he ever had. The past didn't matter and the future wasn't his to know.

It will be foreign no more, Pavel told himself, listening to what felt like he'd always needed to hear, as the bass began to reverberate around the car; this is the thing that has always been missing.

XXX

They had been driving for twenty minutes beyond Moscow's city limits. The snowfall was growing increasingly lighter but Pavel was slowing the car down. Sean noticed that he was on the lookout for something.

'Are we stopping?' he asked.

Pavel didn't reply. He was concentrating. He had managed to follow the directions he'd been given perfectly last time but now the snow made the surroundings appear unfamiliar. He eventually spotted the old wire fence he remembered from before and used it to guide the car to the side road he'd been looking for. From there the road was fenced on both sides. Sean leaned forward to peer more closely through the window and the snow.

Before them stretched half a mile of glistening white wasteland, unblemished by colour. Pavel used the fence as a marker to keep the car close to whatever track lay beneath the snow. A series of grey-bricked buildings slowly emerged from the glare. They seemed disused and abandoned from the outside but, as the snow fell less and less, dense pillars of industrial smoke, ascending like volcanic ash, gradually came into view.

A few hundred metres from the building they passed the end of the fence. Pavel stopped the car, turned off the engine and the music died with it. Sean felt sick. Pavel turned to him.

'Where is papers Grechko gave you?' he asked.

'Why have we stopped?' asked Sean.

Pavel gripped the steering wheel as hard as he could and closed his eyes. The moment he began to think, he removed his seat belt and opened the door.

'Where are you going?' asked Sean.

Pavel said nothing but got out, leaving his door open. A freezing wind blew into the car. Sean reached across and pulled the door shut. He sat up and looked round to find Pavel standing at his window.

'What in the hell are you doing?' he shouted, trying to make himself heard through the glass and the wind.

He saw Pavel reach inside his jacket. Sean went for the buckle of his seat belt, he was breathing quickly and shallowly. He couldn't control his fingers well enough to unfasten his belt. He grew more and more frustrated. He held his breath to stop the tears coming but they did before he breathed again. He heard a tap on the glass. There was the barrel of a gun against the window.

Pavel closed his eyes as much as he could without completely blurring his vision. He could see that Sean had raised his hands and he could hear the words he screamed but he did not know what they meant. I'm trading one life for another, he told himself. You're the free man that I'll become, he whispered to Sean, and you'll be resurrected in my father's name. He held the thought and squeezed the trigger.

Afraid to look and see if he'd missed, he took two steps back from the door and raised his gun again. He closed his eyes completely and fired, again and again, until the sound of the pin hitting an empty chamber was all he could hear.

XXXI

Pavel stood in silence, oblivious to the rising winds and the snow that had begun to fall more heavily. He slowly opened his eyes and looked down through the window at Sean's twisted body. The thought popped into his head that the position Sean was in looked uncomfortable, and he had to close his eyes again as the absurdity of it caught up with him. He turned away from the car, crouched down and touched the ground for balance. The snow was deep. It covered his hand and the tops of his boots. His mouth flooded with saliva. His stomach heaved a little but nothing came up. He spat into the snow and wiped his eyes.

He could see a black saloon similar to his gradually moving towards him. It had emerged unnoticed by him from behind one of the outbuildings near the factory. Its wheels slowly crunched through the snow and pulled up at an angle, close to his crouching figure, shielding him from the wind. The passenger door was pushed open from the inside and Pavel got in. He was grateful for the shelter, but more than that, he yearned for the reassurances he was sure that Suley would make.

His emotions lay like the wreckage of a car, collapsed, broken and distorted. Suley lit a cigarette and passed it to him. He drew the smoke down to the bottom of his lungs and held it there for as long as he could. Blue smoke filled up the car while Suley's occasional glances eventually culminated in a long and searching stare of his passenger. Pavel's shoulders were hunched and his hands were dark red from the snow. They rubbed his knees and occasionally one hand would bring the cigarette to his mouth and linger while he took another draw. Suley found it hard to summon any pity with the sound of gunshots still ringing in his ears, but it saddened him greatly to see his friend like this.

'There's no point in feeling sorry,' said Suley.

Pavel didn't respond.

'For him or for yourself. There is no point.'

Suley knocked the ash from his cigarette and shifted in his seat.

'What's done is done. You have to make the best of it now.'

They weren't the words Suley had planned but the ones he had seemed inappropriate, so he hid behind the anonymity of clichés.

Suddenly, Pavel snatched at the handle, put all his weight behind the door and fell out into the snow. He landed on his hands and began to vomit. Suley turned away. It took a couple of minutes for Pavel to quell his stomach and haul himself back into the car.

'What did you do with the papers?' Suley asked, once Pavel had calmed down.

'They're in the car,' he replied. 'He didn't give them to me.'

Knowing he would have to fetch the papers himself, Suley stepped out into the freezing wind. He unfolded his scarf far enough to cover his ears. Pavel's car was already white with snow, the engine too cold to melt it, and a drift had begun to build up on the passenger side. Suley reached into his pockets and pulled out his gloves.

The passenger window was completely gone and a thin layer of snow had fallen on the capsized rear of the Irishman. At the top of the hip the snow was red with the blood. Suley glanced unintentionally over the rest of the corpse. There was more than one other wound. There was bone where there should have been flesh and the young man's mouth had been torn apart. He lay gawping on the seat as though frozen in time. His eye open, his teeth shattered.

Suley stood up straight, cursed his wandering eyes, made fists with his hands and looked up. It seemed necessary to look up, towards some heavenly place.

Pavel sat listening to the hum of the engine, watching Suley gradually disappearing behind the snow that fell on the windscreen, until the wipers cleared the window once more. He could see that Suley was leaning into the other car and rummaging for the papers. He was glad of his intervention. It left him with a surreal sense that that whole mess had nothing to do with him, that he was a bystander, the witness to an act he couldn't have committed himself.

He wound down his window as Suley approached his door. He felt better for having been sick and now his body seemed able to carry out the instructions he gave it.

'Everything's there. I suggest you go,' said Suley.

He put his hand through the open window and firmly gripped Pavel's shoulder, gently rocking him back and forth as if to wake him.

'Your things are in the boot and your money is under the seat.'

'This isn't for money,' said Pavel.

'I never thought it was.'

Suley tried to put some compassion into his voice.

'Now go. Stop wasting your time. There's nothing you can do here.'

'The body,' said Pavel.

'I'll do as we said,' replied Suley.

Pavel shuffled over to the driver's seat and put the car back into gear. He pulled away, leaving everything behind him.

XXXII

As always, Grechko was at his desk by the time Anna arrived for work. Making the most of her time while she waited for the kettle to boil, she stood over the office heater and held out her shirt so that the heat would rise against her skin. As soon as the kettle boiled, she dropped her shirt and rushed across the room to warm her hands in the steam. If anything, she thought to herself, these mornings are getting colder.

Grechko was on the telephone when Anna took him in his morning coffee. His eyes looked puffy as though he'd had a bad night's sleep and to judge from his sullen expression, she guessed he was for once on the receiving end of orders. She set the coffee down within his reach but didn't look for any sign of gratitude. She closed the door behind her and thought it best if she find some work to get on with.

The morning passed by slowly, not least because typing was her least favourite job, and that was all she could find to do. She read from pages of Grechko's handwriting and typed them onto official paper. It was twelve o'clock before she saw him. Whenever the phone had rung it had gone straight through to his office. She hadn't taken a single outside call all morning, nor had he buzzed her through to his office, not even for more coffee. She knew something was wrong.

'Can I see you in my office for a minute?' Grechko asked,

when he finally emerged, walking over to the cupboard by the kettle and taking a packet of cigarettes for himself. Such self-sufficiency was completely out of character and alarmed Anna. She stood up from her desk and went into his office. Grechko followed her in.

'What's happened?' she asked, before either of them had sat down. She didn't like to wait when she knew bad news was coming. 'Is it something I've done?'

'No,' said Grechko, 'it's nothing like that. We're going to have some visitors this afternoon and they'll want to talk to you as well as me. They're going to ask you about Pavel.'

'Has something happened?'

'There's no need to worry but we need to get a few things straight before they arrive. Now, you know what the rules of conduct between us should be, don't you?' Anna nodded. 'In that case, you know that I trust you with more information than I should.' Anna nodded again. 'So, we have to be clear on what you know. Tell me what you know about Pavel's last trip and we'll decide what's safe to tell them.'

'Is he alright?' she asked.

'He's fine. What do you know about the trip?'

Anna thought for a moment, trying to recall any arrangements she had made on his behalf.

'Nothing, really. He made most of his own arrangements,' she said.

'What do you mean, he made his own?'

'Yes, he's been doing that quite a lot lately.'

'You didn't think that was odd?'

'No, he said it was your idea.'

'So you have no idea where he is?'

'Ireland, I presume. That young man was Irish, wasn't he?'

'Don't presume anything!' shouted Grechko.

His frayed temper had snapped. He pushed back his chair and stood up.

'Do you have any idea at all where he was going or how he intended on getting there?'

'No,' Anna replied. 'But isn't that better for both of us? If I don't know anything I'm not supposed to?'

'I suppose,' sighed Grechko.

He got up from his chair and went to the window.

'So where is he?' asked Anna.

'We don't know,' replied Grechko, 'but don't repeat that.'

'What do you mean?'

'He's gone, and so has the shipment.'

'You mean he's defected?' Anna asked in a whisper.

'I'd say so,' said Grechko, 'wouldn't you?'

She stood up without replying and left the room. She tread as softly as she could and pulled the door closed behind her. She went back to her desk and resumed her typing but soon lost her place on the page.

She took a tissue from the box on her desk and walked to the window. There was snow on the window ledge but the courtyard had turned to sludge overnight. The frozen tracks of Pavel's tyres could still be seen. They ran from the middle of the courtyard and out of the gates. My God, she thought, you are a clever boy.

XXXIII

As Pavel expected, 1989 was a difficult year and any contact with Martina was impossible. He wondered if she ever really grasped the nature of his work, or the regret and guilt it caused him. If she couldn't forgive him he wouldn't blame her but he hoped she might try to understand. If Suley had taken the time to visit her, like Pavel had asked him to, he knew his friend would have tried to explain. There was money for her, but as for the promises about the house, he didn't know what would happen. He wasn't in a position to write her a letter and he wouldn't have known what to say.

Most of that year he spent in southern Europe. Travel had been the essence of his profession but there was novelty in the crossing of each new border out of choice. He never stayed in one place for longer than his nerves could bear, three or four days at the most. He travelled through Italy and the Greek islands. He spent two months wandering the French Riviera, and then he moved south to explore Spain.

As Christmas approached he made tracks, via Paris, for London, where he felt the safest he had felt all year. He could go out onto the streets and lose himself in the hordes of all-day shoppers. Every day, he would buy himself something new and sit with his bags and a drink in a different pub, as nondescript as the next man.

He knew that London could, if he wished, mark the end of his nomadic existence. He had a contact who could put him in touch with Suley. He knew his friend would be here for Christmas as he was every year, but he decided to wait until the festivities were over before he tried his luck. He didn't like the idea of having to go through a third party but it had been at Suley's insistence.

He sat through Christmas suffering the television in his hotel room. He filled the room up with flowers to keep him company. And he tried on the new clothes he had bought, attempting to mould a new image for himself. He could hardly remember what his reflection had looked like on the morning he left his Moscow flat. Since then, his skin had taken on what looked like a permanent darkness from so many days in the sun. His hair was cropped and, when he gently brushed the crown of his head, he could feel the hair thinning. He had lost enough weight to make the bones in his features more prominent. Now, with a carefully shaped beard and new clothes, he was almost unrecognisable to himself. Staring back from the mirror was an unfamiliar face, but one far easier to confront.

XXXIV

'What can I get you?' asked the barman.

Pavel sat at the bar and pencilled out requests for Suley.

'A pint of lager, please,' said Pavel.

'It's a bit late for Christmas shopping, isn't it?' the barman said, nodding towards Pavel's bags.

'It's all for me.'

'On your holidays then?'

'Yes.'

He felt good to be part of a spontaneous conversation.

'Where are you from?'

Pavel paused and smiled, seeing no danger in honesty.

'Prague,' he replied, 'not there but near.'

'Czechoslovakia!' the barman exclaimed, raising his eyebrows.

'That's right,' Pavel replied, unable to see what was so extraordinary about that.

'Wow,' the barman said, taking his money. 'Must be a funny feeling for you today.'

Pavel tilted his head to one side in confusion. He couldn't see what was so amusing in being Czech. He took his change, smiled and shrugged his shoulders. The barman leaned slightly towards the bar.

'You don't watch the news, do you?'

Another customer called the barman away but before he walked off he pointed over Pavel's head to a corner of the room.

A television in the corner was showing pictures of Prague and a huge crowd that had gathered in Wenceslas Square. There was a sea of faces in front of the National Museum and people stood on the balconies, waving to the crowd. Pavel jumped off his seat and approached the television.

'More sound,' he shouted excitedly back to the barman. 'I can't hear.'

The barman was out of earshot and the television was out of reach. Pavel grabbed his bags and fled for the door, leaving his drink untouched. He spotted a taxi and stepped into the road. He held out his hand and watched the driver's eyes until they met his.

'Charlotte Street, please,' he said, getting into the cab. 'Please be fast.'

'I can only go as fast as the traffic, mate,' replied the driver.

'Please be fast,' Pavel repeated, talking to the cars outside.

Back in his room Pavel flicked through the channels with one hand and thumbed through a television guide with the other. Eventually he found a news programme scheduled to start in ten minutes time. He found the right station and went to the mini bar. As he poured himself a drink he tried to calm down. He couldn't remember the last time he had heard any news to speak of. He hadn't recognised any of the faces on the balconies of the Museum but perhaps in his excitement he hadn't been looking properly. The worst he could imagine was Gorbachev's face filling the screen, cut to running riots and burnt-out cars littering the city. Expect the worst, Pavel told himself, trying to hold the image in his head and bury the glimmer of hope.

He watched the news sitting on the end of his bed. When the main feature finished he lay back and closed his eyes. Somehow, amid Christmas, his compatriots had found the time to elect themselves a president. Six weeks before that, they had marched through the city to Wenceslas Square and stayed there. They had sung through the night. Some had lit candles and sung old Czech songs and those that knew the words had joined in. Some had sung John Lennon's 'Give Peace a Chance', and again, those that knew the words had joined in. Some answered questions from the police and others chose to run. Some showed the police their bare backside and then tried to run. Of those who preferred to stay and fight, most took a beating.

And then, as though it had simply taken them twenty years to realise they were not welcome, the Warsaw troops gathered their things to leave. The news said that not a single shot had been fired.

Lost in his own world Pavel had missed seeing the real one change. Lying back on the bed he didn't even try to stop himself from crying. All he could think about was home. He was a citizen of Czechoslovakia. A free country.

XXXV

On Suley's advice Pavel didn't return home straight away. His immediate future still lay in London. Suley found him a place to live and he began to gradually reacquaint himself with life's routines. He knew the money wasn't going to last forever. Suley began to find him jobs of the only nature he knew, using the only skills he had. No more than two years passed from the day Czechoslovakia liberated itself, to the day that the country he was running from ceased to exist.

Loneliness grew in him like a tumour, never fading. He would go to Trafalgar Square and feed the pigeons, stretching out his arms to make a perch for the birds and make himself as visible as possible. Someone surely would see him, and know who he was.

After eighteen months, he made his inevitable call to Suley.

'I'm going home,' he told him. 'When you want me, you'll find me in Prague.'

In the view from the window of his home, the Vltava flowed from right to left. She went where she pleased, unconcerned and uncontrolled by whoever occupied her banks. He could sit by the window, watching day turn into night and back again, when the starless sky ebbed back like the tide, leaving morning in its wake. He shared something in common with the river. More than he had ever dared hope for.

XXXVI

He had been watching the road from the window for an hour, mistaking each car that passed for Alex's taxi. When it finally arrived, he sat down at his desk and tried to adopt a casual pose. Seeing the flowers he'd bought the day before on the dining room table, he rushed across and took them, in their vase, through to the kitchen sink. He folded the flowers in half at the stems and pushed them down into the bin. He poured the water down the sink and put the vase into a cupboard. When he'd finished, he hurried back to his desk. Alex came in and dropped his bag and coat at the door and went to the sofa.

'Welcome home, Alex,' said Dominik.

'No place like it.'

He cut a more imposing figure now, thought Dominik. The last few months of exercise had had an effect on Alex's shape that he hadn't noticed until now. He had grown blind to what he saw every day.

Dominik went through to the kitchen and got them a beer each while Alex collapsed on the sofa. Only with a drink in his hand, Dominik thought, would Alex talk about Vienna.

'To be honest with you,' he began, 'I'll feel guilty if Suley still wants to pay me.'

'Have you spoken with him?'

Alex nodded.

'About half an hour after I'd spoken to you this morning. He said sorry about the meeting in St Vitus. He said he was late but I wasn't there. Anyway, I had to come back by coach in the end but I haven't got a clue who it was I was meant to be following.'

Dominik took a sip of his drink.

'Then he didn't tell it to you.'

'He said it didn't matter. So long as I was on the right coach I just had to tell him if we were searched at the border.'

'And you were?'

'No. Someone came on board to check our passports but that was it. It took ten minutes, if that.'

'And then what?'

'I rang Suley from the station as soon as I was off the coach. He just said thanks, good job. He said he'd be in touch. Have you spoken to him?'

Dominik shook his head. Alex shrugged his shoulders and took a sip of his beer.

'So, that's the end of the adventure, is it?' asked Dominik.

'Looks like it.'

'Everything to normal.'

It was clear from Dominik's expression that he expected some kind of response. All Alex could manage was a sigh.

'What would you call normal?' he asked.

'We must be back to the way things are before,' Dominik replied. 'What you think? You still have much to learn, Alex. This is only the beginning.'

'That's what worries me,' said Alex. 'Perhaps I shouldn't waste any more of your time. I could leave now before I do something I regret.'

'Leave where? Here? Where would you go?'

'I don't know.'

'You haven't thought about it.'

'I haven't had time to think,' said Alex. 'That's my problem in a nutshell. I haven't had time to think.'

'What will you do?' Dominik asked, dreading what conclusions Alex might have reached on his own.

'I need peace and quiet,' he replied, looking into his glass. 'What do you suggest?'

Alex sat in silence.

'Why don't you go to the country? Use the house for a few days,' asked Dominik.

Alex looked up, hoping that the relief wouldn't show on his face.

'Alone, Alex. Go on your own. If it's peace and quiet you want, Dubá will feel like paradise.'

'How would I get there?'

'You can take the car,' replied Dominik.

He stood up and walked over to the bookshelves and began to run his finger along the spines of a collection of maps. He pulled one out and passed it over to Alex. 'It's north of Prague. It should only take you hour to drive.'

Alex unfolded the map and spread it out on the floor, trying to keep his enthusiasm in check.

'You can go tomorrow,' said Dominik. 'Make weekend of it.'

'You don't mind me going?' Alex asked, turning his full attention to Dominik.

'The sooner you get some rest, the better for us both,' he replied.

'Perhaps that's all I need. Before things get out of hand.'

'What you mean?' asked Dominik.

'Well, I haven't broken the law yet. That's going to be a big step for me.'

'You break the law everyday. Same as everybody else.'

'Maybe, but I never intend to.'

'Does that make such a difference?'

'Yes it does.'

'Well, that's your choice,' said Dominik.

He took their empty bottles from the table and stood up.

'But please don't think of me like the common criminal. We don't all choose the life we lead.'

Alex hurried to his feet and followed Dominik through to the kitchen.

'I didn't call you a common criminal. Stop twisting my words. You can't expect me to apologise for having had the right to make my own decisions.'

'I wouldn't know anything about it,' said Dominik.

'A fat lot of good it did me,' said Alex.

Dominik took a towel to dry his hands, wet from rinsing the bottles, and smiled placidly. He glanced up to the clock on the kitchen wall.

'Seven o'clock!' he exclaimed with mock surprise. 'You must be hungry.'

Alex accepted the truce.

'I'll have a quick shower,' he said.

Alex grabbed his bag and ran up the stairs.

'Hurry up!' Dominik called after him.

He took a brown, leather-bound notebook from his desk and took a seat by the window. He wouldn't mind the wait if he could see the river. He found the page on which he'd last been working, unclipped his pen from the spine of the book and read what he'd most recently written.

When the first settlers of Prague declared their journey over, and the banks of Vltava their land long promised, they did well to keep their distance from the river. At the whim of nature, her waters could turn ferocious, and it wasn't until the tenth century AD that a wooden bridge was constructed. It united the banks of Malá Strana with the Old Town and deluded the citizens into thinking that the river had been tamed. In 1157 the Vltava showed them otherwise when she took the bridge with her on her way downstream.

His eyes were drawn to bridge, as yellow as sand in the fading sunlight. He read on.

Determined as ever to cross swords with nature, people immediately set about building a bridge of stone. Three years in the making, it seemed that Judith Bridge would be able to withstand the river's temper and, for a time, the river acknowledged their efforts. It was nearly two

hundred years before Judith Bridge would go the way of her predecessor
and follow the floodwaters north.

Eventually, on the 13th July 1357, at a time stipulated by the royal
astrologers, Charles IV stepped up to lay the initial stones of what would
come to be known as Charles Bridge. This time the bridge was over
twenty years in the making, and finally met with Vltava's approval.
Not until the people had built a bridge that befitted their river's beauty
did the waters begin to calm.

Dominik closed his eyes and settled back into his chair. The
calming of the waters led to a marriage between city and river,
he thought, which surpassed the bonds of human nature. It's
impossible to tell which defines the other's shape. The river
would not follow the path it does were it not for the shape of the
land, and the land would not be the shape it is were it not for the
flow of the river. And this city, he thought, this city grew from
the river the day the first boat docked. Or, perhaps, the day the
first fish was caught from the bank. Dominik rubbed his eyes
and went back to the page.

City and river belong to each other, he wrote in his book.

At times, Dominik could feel the serenity of the river venture
beyond its banks to explore the city and, when he did, he awoke
unaided by dreams or clocks or early-morning commotion. The
mid-morning light would galvanise the colours of the room. The
books that lined his shelves seem to lay open their knowledge,
rather than simply ornament his walls. Serenity was on him now,
as he sat with his thoughts of the river and her bridge. When he
heard the faint sound of running water coming from the bathroom, he smiled in the knowledge that Alex was home.

Upstairs, Alex had drawn the shower curtain across the bath
and started the water on full power to drown out the sound of
his voice. He took Dominik's phone from his bag and perched
himself on the edge of the sink. He had already memorised
Olina's number but still took out the card she had written it on.

He had no mistrust of his memory but he preferred to read the number from the paper she had touched. As usual, he counted the rings of her phone until her voice interrupted.

'Prosim.'

'Olina, it's me, Alex,' he said.

'It is raining in Vienna?' she asked.

'I wouldn't know, I'm in Prague,' he replied. 'I'm just getting in the shower.'

'You're naked?' she asked.

'Well,' Alex paused for a moment and walked to the middle of the room. 'Yes, I am,' he lied.

She was silent. He smiled, wondering what pictures were running through her mind.

'Hello?'

'Hello,' she replied.

'I was wondering what you were doing at the weekend.'

'Why?'

'I thought you might like to come to the country with me.'

'Where?'

'To a cottage. It's in a village called Dubá. Do you know where it is?' he asked.

'What is cottage?'

'A house, in the country.'

'I've never heard of it,' Olina replied.

'Well, I have the cottage for the weekend and a car to get us there, so what do you say?'

'I say yes.'

Her reply was quick and quiet but to Alex it sounded like singing.

He changed his clothes and wet his hair before presenting himself downstairs.

That night he and Dominik walked to the centre of the city, rather than visiting any of their local haunts. It seemed to reflect their changing situation. Throughout the evening they conversed more like acquaintances than the friends they supposed they were. But neither could tell themselves why.

XXXVII

The next morning Alex came down to a note on the breakfast table, weighted down by the keys to the car and an old iron key, to the house in Dubá, he presumed.

Some of us cannot spend morning in bed. Address is on back of map. Map is in car. I'll see you when you come home.

Alex sighed heavily when he read the note. He felt, had Dominik underlined the word home, he couldn't have been more obvious.

For the rest of the morning Alex slowly packed what he would need for the weekend. He eventually left with a few hours to spare, planning to drive around the city and familiarise himself with the car before he picked up Olina.

The car smelt new and familiar inside. The colour of the dashboard and the grey leather upholstery all made it look like the same car Dominik had driven in London. That seemed like a long time ago to him.

He crossed the bridge into New Town and went south to Vyšehrad. He drove slowly at first, constantly reminding himself which side of the road he should be on. When he'd gained enough confidence he followed the signs on Pankrácké Náměstí and pulled on to the fast road that went back into the city. The traffic was very quick and he made himself concentrate on the road while cars skimmed past his window. He found it hard to use the mirrors with cars driving so close to one another.

Without warning, the ground beneath the road fell away and the road became a bridge that spanned a valley. He had seen this bridge from the ground but never from the top. Dominik had told him how it had been christened Suicide Bridge from the sheer numbers of people who jumped. He could feel his stomach sinking and his legs felt light. He gripped the steering wheel tightly until he had passed to the other side. As soon as he could he pulled off of the main road and found himself in Vinohrady. He drove the car very slowly around the block and looked for a place to stop.

He parked at the side of a road from where he could watch St Vitus. The sky was grey up above but blue on the horizon. He waited for a sense of paranoia to take hold. It didn't happen. A tram rung its bell as it passed the car. He restarted the engine and drove away.

Close to Olina's office he found a space for the car. Flicking through the CDs he found in the glove box, he looked for something Czech he could use to impress Olina. He was still undecided when she tapped on the window.

'You're travelling light,' he said, taking her bag.

She was dressed all in black and it accentuated the olive colour of her skin.

'Did nobody tell you that the summer is over?'

'I don't believe it.'

'You'll be after my jumpers.'

She raised her hand, placing it onto his cheek. She moved onto the tips of her toes and, enticing him to meet her half way, kissed him on the lips for as long as her balance permitted.

'We shall go?' she asked.

'The door's open,' he replied.

Olina walked round to the passenger door. He was excited by her impatience to leave. He put her bag into the boot of the car as fast as he could.

Alex laid the map on Olina's lap.

'Are you able to navigate?' he asked.

'How you say?'

'Navigate,' he repeated, hoping the map itself would be explanation enough for what it meant.

'Left, right, straight ahead. I can do it.'

As they made their way out of the city Alex prepared to deliver a false account of his trip to Vienna, but as long as he waited, Olina didn't ask.

XXXVIII

The people they stopped in the Village Square greeted the address on the back of Dominik's note with blank expressions. Armed with the note and the map Olina went to ask in the nearest shop.

The flaking plaster on the shop front, the tinned food displayed in the window or the broken cobbles on the pavement outside could have belonged to any decade in the last ten. Acres of trees followed the roads that led away from the village. Their colours ran from green to gold and red, as far as Alex could see.

Four children stood around their bikes on the village green. Alex watched the noisiest of the four and tried to picture Dominik on the green as a child. He found it hard to believe that he came from a place like this. What is it about a place like this that makes a man like that, he asked himself. The village seemed so still and peaceful.

'It's five-minute to drive from here,' Olina announced, jumping back into the car.

'Which way?' asked Alex.

Olina pointed to the opposite side of the square.

The house was set back from the road at the edge of a valley covered in forest. Alex stopped the car by the garden gate, covered in the same ivy that smothered the fence. Olina forgot about the bags and went to explore.

The buildings closest to the gate were sheds that led onto a small outbuilding. Next to those was a large white house with small wooden shutters on the windows.

'It's bigger than I expect,' said Olina.

'It's nicer than I expected,' replied Alex.

He took the old iron key and tried it in the lock. Instead of following him inside, Olina walked around the house and further into the garden that sloped down the hill.

Alex wandered through the house, room by room. The ceilings were low and crossed by beams from wall to wall. At each doorway he needed to duck his head. He searched the dressers and mantelpieces for old family photographs, wondering how quickly, if at all, he could recognise Dominik as a child, and what features might have prevailed through time. By the time he reached the kitchen, had the key not fitted the lock, he would have doubted whether he had the right house. The kitchen was the last room he found and there hadn't been a single piece of evidence to suggest that the house had ever been lived in.

There was a knock on the window from Olina. He reached over the sink and unlatched the window.

'Come see,' she said, before walking back across the patio and down the garden.

The back door was locked so he left the house the way he had entered. Olina was waving from the bottom of the garden. She was standing in a corner, in the shade of a willow tree.

'What have you found?' he asked.

Olina pointed to a gravestone close to the base of the tree. He wrapped his arms around her shoulders and read the grave's inscription.

'Read it to me,' he whispered as she rested her head on his arm.

'With the memory of Dominik Rubín, Jana Rubínová, April 5th 1930 - 19th August 1988.'

'In loving memory,' Alex said, correcting her English.

'No, that's not what it saying. It say, "with the memory," and there aren't date for him. It's strange.'

'I didn't know he was named after his father.'

'Dominik?'

'Yes, Rubín's his last name. This must be his parents' grave.'

'Did you know them?' she asked, turning to face him but careful not to break the frame of his arms. He shook his head.

Every time he saw her, the subtlest detail seemed to have changed. He could never tell how, but each time she seemed new and different and better. Her eyes, which not only looked different from each other, looked different in daylight than in the night-time, and different in the sunshine than in shadow.

He held the sides of her face and stepped close towards her. She stretched up to kiss his mouth with more force than he had expected. When they broke their kiss they held each other. She shivered from the cold. He tightened his hold and pulled her in as close as he could.

'Aren't you going to show me house?'

Olina broke his hold and took one of his hands in both of hers. She tugged him gently and Alex followed her back to the house.

He led her through the rooms he had explored alone. She found something she liked in each room, whether it was the colour of a cushion or the view from a window, and complimented it as though it owed its appeal to his taste. At the top of the house, in a bedroom that looked out onto the woods, Olina perched herself on the edge of the bed and declared it the best room yet.

'I'll put your bag in here then, shall I?' asked Alex.

He went to look at the view and leant upon the windowsill.

'You can see a lake from here,' he said.

He heard her stand but he didn't turn around.

He felt his shirt move before she laid her hand on the skin of his back. Her touch was like a journey's end. He closed his eyes and dropped his head. His only concern lay within that room.

XXXIX

Through the open gap in the bedroom window a cold morning breeze flurried across Alex's shoulders. It took a moment while he gazed at the window to fathom where he was, and another moment to realise he was alone. He reached across the empty half of the bed and anxiously listened out for any signs of life. When he heard footsteps in the kitchen, he laid his head back on the pillow.

They had left it too late to restock the cupboards the night before, and by the time hunger had seized them, too late to cook. They had taken the car back into the village looking for somewhere to eat and found a small hotel just off the green that had served them beer and fried cheese. They had stayed until midnight.

Conversation had come easily. There were moments it had felt hard to talk about one thing at a time and not let all the words come at once. There were also times when the words seemed to matter less and silence said more. It was at those times, he thought, he had felt the indefinable word of love slowly unveiling its meaning.

The stairs creaked and Alex propped himself up in the bed. Olina came in wearing the jumper he had discarded the night before, carrying two cups in her hands. She smiled when she found him awake and watching her.

'I find coffee in kitchen,' she said, handing him a cup.

She placed her cup on the bedside table while she climbed back onto the bed, and then took it up to drink. He looked at his watch and blew on the surface of his coffee.

'Ten o'clock,' he said. 'I'm getting lazy.'

'Yes you are. I've been up for half the hour.'

He put his coffee to one side and laid his head on her legs.

'Have you always been such an early riser?' he asked mockingly.

'The phone don't let me sleep.'

Alex lay still for a moment.

'Your phone?' he asked her.

'I don't have my phone.'

He sat up quickly, nearly spilling her coffee and fixed her with a look of bewilderment.

'What phone?'

'The phone downstairs,' she replied, looking confused. 'It ring all morning.'

'Did you answer it?'

'Yes.'

'Who was it?'

'Dominik,' she said.

Alex swept his arm out from under him and collapsed back onto the pillows. He stared blankly at the ceiling.

'Was there a message?' he asked.

'He ask if you call him. I told him you are asleep.'

'He didn't want to know who you were?' asked Alex.

'No,' she replied. 'Is that why you worry? He doesn't know I'm here?'

'Don't be silly,' he said. 'I'm just wondering what he wants. Maybe he needs me back at work.'

'No!' Olina protested. 'What you say if he does?'

'I'll say no.'

He pulled back the sheets and got out of bed while Olina returned to her coffee, happy with his answer. He put on the clothes that he found on the floor.

'Where you going?' Olina asked, covering her legs with the sheets.

'I may as well tell him now,' he said, pulling the door shut as he left the room.

Despite the unknown consequences Alex couldn't help feeling some relief as he descended the stairs. He took a firm grip of the phone and slowly dialled what seemed like Dominik's number rather than theirs. He didn't count the rings but hoped they'd go on forever.

'Prosím.'

'I hear you rang,' said Alex.

'It wasn't important,' Dominik replied. 'I just wanted to know that you found the house, but now I know.'

'I should have rung you. I'm sorry.'

Dominik laughed.

'You don't have to check in. You're not child.'

'Her name is Olina. I was going to tell you about her when we got back.'

'Are you paying her?'

'What?'

'Are you paying for her company?' Dominik repeated.

'Fuck off,' said Alex.

'It would make things easier if you were.'

'Well, I'm not, so get that idea out of your head.'

'So, we have to find out who she is.'

'It has nothing to do with you.'

'It has everything to do with me!' Dominik's voice exploded in Alex's ear. 'I have to know who she is.'

'I know who she is!'

'All you know is what she told you. How do you know the truth?'

'Because I trust her,' Alex said, defiantly. 'Because I love her.'

'That's been a good secret.'

'Can you blame me, if this is how you react? You're totally paranoid. I don't want to end up like you.'

He regretted his words but couldn't bring himself to apologise. It would have made them seem worse. There was silence on the other end of the phone.

'Are you still there?' asked Alex.

'Yes,' Dominik replied.

'I'll be back tomorrow evening. We'll sort everything out then.'

Alex waited to hear the line go dead before he hung up the phone himself.

XL

The radio was poor substitute for company and it wasn't long before Dominik reached for the phone again and dialled Suley's number. They arranged to meet in an hour's time. Unsettled in the stillness of his flat, Dominik left as soon as he could.

The streets were not as crowded as they had been through the summer but the tourists still came all year round. It bewildered Dominik that they would be fewest in the heart of winter, when the city looked her best, dressed head to toe in flakes of snow, each one gleaming the colour of the moon. Perhaps this winter, he thought, the river would retire beneath a blanket of ice to sleep through the worst of the cold.

He found a quiet table at the river café on Kampa Island and ordered a beer. He turned his attention to the river and watched people steer their paddleboats to and from the opposite bank. A few children dressed in heavy winter coats stared down at the water from the bridge, waiting to see whose stick would emerge first.

He saw Suley at the café door. When he approached the table, Dominik forced a smile and sat up straight in his chair. Suley took a seat and ordered a tea.

'You don't look so good,' he said.

'Things aren't so good.'

'Can't we go inside?' Suley asked, feeling the chill of the

breeze that blew off the river. Dominik huddled deeper into his coat and slouched back into his chair. Suley resigned himself to the cold.

'What's the problem?' he asked.

'Alex.'

'Ah.'

'You don't look surprised.'

'What's he done?'

'He's met a girl. He says he's in love.'

Suley's expression didn't change.

'So, what's the problem?' Suley asked again. 'He's young. That's what they do best.'

'I'm serious,' snapped Dominik. 'I don't know who she is, what she does. She could be anyone.'

'Then chances are she's harmless.' Suley shrugged his shoulders and smiled, suggesting that Dominik had just quelled his own suspicions.

'I need to know. You find out for me.'

Suley leaned in towards the table.

'You want them followed. Is that what you're saying?'

'Whatever you like. Just find out.'

'If it's so important to you.'

Suley thanked the waitress for his tea. Then he buried his hands deep into his jacket pockets.

'You think I'm being paranoid,' said Dominik.

'No, I don't think you're paranoid,' he replied. 'You have every right to be, above all people, but I don't think that.'

'Careful,' said Dominik. 'I'm just being careful.'

'I wouldn't say careful either. I'd say that you were being jealous.'

'Of Alex.'

Dominik forced a laugh.

'I don't know,' Suley continued. 'Of Alex, of her. Maybe you're jealous of them both.'

'And what exactly would I be jealous for?' asked Dominik.

'Why did you bring Alex here?'

'What are you talking about?'

'What is he doing here? Why did you bring him to Prague?'

'He was lost. I thought I could teach him something.'

'No, no, my friend. I'm not as naïve as he is,' said Suley. 'I don't believe that.'

'Well, why do you think?' asked Dominik.

'It's not his fault if you're lonely.'

'You think I bring him here, put him through everything, just for some company?'

Again, Suley shrugged his shoulders and offered no reply. He wouldn't answer the question for him.

'You're the fool as he is,' said Dominik.

'He must be a fool to have followed you here, but he doesn't know you like I do. I think that's why I'm sorry for him. It's you I find hard to understand.'

Dominik didn't respond. He stared out at the river. Suley stood up to go.

'You will find out who she is?' asked Dominik.

Suley nodded then walked away.

XLI

It was about halfway down the cup that Konstantin began to gamble with his coffee. Knowing that half an inch of sediment lay at the bottom of his cup he refined himself to careful sips. He fiddled with his hat, persistently pulling it down at the edges and running his fingers along the hem, checking that the wire leading to his earphone wasn't showing.

'Stop playing with it,' a voice said through his earpiece. Konstantin felt for the microphone in his sleeve and, pretending to yawn, spoke into it.

'Who's that?'

'I'm on the bridge,' Peter said, knowing that his voice would be recognised the second time around. 'I'm waving at you.'

Konstantin looked across to Charles Bridge from the river café veranda where he was chancing his luck with a Turkish coffee. Halfway along the bridge he saw Peter, his arm in the air.

'I can see you,' Konstantin said, surprised with himself.

'Well, for God's sake don't wave back,' said Peter. 'He's on his way.'

'Then why are you on the bridge?' asked Konstantin.

'In case they go anywhere else. He's wearing black trousers, a brown suede jacket and a grey scarf.'

'What does he look like again?' Konstantin asked, deadpan. The temptation to test Peter's temper was too much for him.

'He's coming in now. Tell us when he leaves.'

Within a couple of minutes Konstantin had spotted him. He watched him as he made his way to a table at the edge of the veranda, away from the other customers, near the man-made bank of the river. He couldn't help but stare. Once, on his way home from school, he'd seen Serge Bubka running in the park. He had never taken the route through the park before. He took it everyday, there and back, from that day forth, but he never saw him again. It had been divine intervention, he told himself. He'd felt the same confounding excitement then as he felt now. He watched him order and watched him wait, and together he waited with him.

To keep up appearances, Konstantin accepted the offer of another coffee. The first had at least fended off the cold. The waitress brought Konstantin's coffee then moved on to his table to attend the man who had arrived to join him. He was short, portly and middle-aged with skin that looked accustomed to the sun. Their conversation seemed slow and strained. When the waitress came back she began to prepare a tea.

Konstantin wondered if he should inform someone about the new arrival but seeing Peter still on the bridge, he decided against it. They would no doubt know who he was. For all they tell me, he said to himself, he might be one of us. The waitress took over the tea.

The conversation seemed to have reached an awkward pause. They were both staring at the river and words between him and his companion had ceased. There was a parting shot between them or perhaps a forgiving farewell, Konstantin couldn't tell, and then the fleeting visit was over. His companion left him sitting alone.

He sat with his hands in his pockets, slumped in his chair, hypnotised by the water. Eventually he rose to his feet and placed some money under his empty glass. Konstantin's heartbeat quickened. He raised his sleeve to his mouth and spoke quietly.

'He's going. He's left some money and he's going.'

Konstantin's earphone crackled back to life and Peter's breathless voice came through.

'Follow him, slowly. And don't forget to pay.'

Konstantin looked across to the bridge but Peter had gone.

'Where are you?' he asked.

'I'll catch you up,' Peter said, impatiently. He sounded as though he was running. 'Pay your bill and go.'

XLII

Lost in his thoughts, Dominik walked home the way he had gone to the café. It was the first time Suley had voiced any opinion on Alex. He had known about him within a week of his arrival, nearly four months ago to the day. It felt longer than that to Dominik. The summer had condensed itself into one long memory, from which he could distinguish no more than a day, an endless, beautiful day. The days before Alex's arrival felt impossibly distant to him now and their contents no more than a regrettable phase. Suley had said nothing of which Dominik wasn't already unaware. He simply chose not to think about it. He ambled home through Kampa Park.

Peter had caught up with Konstantin and together they followed in his footsteps, always keeping him in sight.

Dominik bent down to the flowerbeds and carefully picked a handful of flowers.

'What's he doing?' asked Konstantin.

'Just keep walking,' replied Peter.

Dominik took the flowers with him and carried on home. They slowed their pace a little and allowed him to open up a lead. It wasn't until Dominik reached into his pocket for his keys that Peter spoke into his sleeve.

'He's coming up,' he said.

Peter heard a brief, incomprehensible reply over his earphone before the line went dead. Dominik walked into the building and out of sight.

'What do we do now?' Konstantin asked, relieved that his moment of responsibility was over.

'Where did you put the car?' asked Peter.

Konstantin pointed across the street to a road that ran perpendicular to the river.

The noise resonated through the hall when Dominik closed the front door behind him and echoed down the stairwell. The lift shaft was empty as usual – someone forgetting to send the cage back down. Dominik called the lift and glanced up to see which floor the culprit lived on. It was his.

He thought about the conversation he and Alex had had earlier that morning. Perhaps his words had made more of an impression than he'd realised. Perhaps Alex missed him too. He hadn't noticed the car parked out on the street, but then he hadn't been expecting to see it. He considered for a moment going back outside to check but, as the lift drew closer, excitement got the better of him. Alex must have come to his senses almost immediately, he thought. He had been gone from the flat for only two hours or so, but that was plenty of time to make the journey back from Dubá. He threw the flowers he had picked into the bin at the foot of the stairs.

As the lift ascended it occurred to him that perhaps she was there too. Maybe Alex had brought her along to reiterate their solidarity. There will be no confrontation, thought Dominik, as he pushed aside the cage doors of the lift and stepped out onto his floor. He would dazzle them both with his unsung capacity for compromise. He jangled his keys to announce his arrival and let himself in.

There were no bags on the floor or coats on the stand, and the flat was as quiet as it had been before he left. Dominik stood just inside the door and called out Alex's name but there was no answer. In an attempt to lure Alex out of the bedroom, where he assumed the two of them had gone, Dominik walked through to the kitchen and noisily prepared to make tea. He was checking to see if the kettle was warm when he heard the front door close.

'Alex,' he called out with relief, hurrying back to the living room.

The first man to catch his eye was standing at the front door, his legs slightly bent, a gun raised in front of him, aimed at Dominik's head.

Dominik looked around the room and counted five other men, each frozen in the same stance. They had come from nowhere, like guests at a surprise party. Dominik looked back to the man at the door.

'Who are you?' he asked.

The man didn't reply but shot a nervous glance to the man by Dominik's desk. He, who looked no older than Alex, lowered his gun, placed it back beneath his jacket and produced a pair of handcuffs.

'Please,' he said. 'Put your hands on your head and turn around.'

Dominik didn't move.

'Who are you?' he asked again, this time addressing the man who had just spoken.

The young man repeated the order with more venom in his voice, but this time he spoke in Russian. Dominik clenched his fists and slowly fell to his knees.

'Bastards,' he whispered to himself.

The young man raised his voice and repeated the order, again in Russian.

'I don't speak your fucking language!' Dominik screamed at the top of his voice.

Once again the order was repeated, this time more calmly.

Dominik lunged for the bottom draw of his desk but the young man blocked his way. Within seconds, he had been pulled from behind down onto the floor and bodies piled on top of him one by one. As he felt the steel clasp around his wrists he winced. He counted the years since he'd left Moscow. They didn't amount to many.

They marched him out of the front door and summoned the lift. He was made to sit on his hands in the corner of the lift and two men rode down with him. More men were waiting at the entrance to the building, watching the street. A black saloon pulled up adjacent to the entrance and one of them opened the rear door. On a given signal Dominik was bundled into the back of the car. The young man who appeared to be in charge and who was still issuing instructions in Russian joined him on the back seat. Dominik could tell it was his native tongue. He hadn't forgotten how they sounded.

'Who are you?' Dominik asked again. He was just pushed into the corner of the seat. The young man took out his gun and pressed it into Dominik's stomach.

The car parked in front of them pulled out into the street and they followed. Dominik looked back over his shoulder. He counted two cars following behind them in convoy.

'VIP,' he remarked, to nobody in particular. He sat back in his seat in silence and watched the city pass by his window.

XLIII

The small convoy crossed Jiráskův Most and took the road
that splits Charles Square in two. At Náměstí Miru the convoy
turned left into Vinohrady. They drove one block and parked
one behind the other. Someone from the front car got out and
began to remove a row of traffic cones from the side of the
road.

'What are we doing?' asked Dominik.

His door was opened from the outside and a barrel–chested
thirty–something covered Dominik's mouth with tape, took
him by the collar, pulled him out from the car and hurried him
into the building.

Dominik tried to memorise his surroundings but the interior
seemed like so many others in Prague. A spiral staircase coiled
around the lift shaft but there was no skylight. Flakes of paint
had fallen from the walls to litter the grey concrete steps. The
light switch hung from the wall by its wires.

A push in the back prompted Dominik up the stairs. A few
men who had been following took the lead and ushered him
down the hallway to a door on the forth floor that was already
open.

Peter stood at the threshold watching Dominik approach.
It was the first time he'd seen him up close. He'd been shown
innumerable photographs but those photos had all been old.

It took time to match the physical features before him to the frozen images he had seen from the past, like the recognition of someone famous. Here was a face without a voice. Peter placed his hand on Dominik's shoulder and made a grateful gesture to the rest of the entourage. He ushered Dominik into the room, removed the tape from his mouth and closed the door.

'Dominik,' Grechko said, getting up out of his chair and moving away from the window. 'That's what you call yourself these days, isn't it?'

Dominik didn't reply. It had taken him a few seconds to recognise the old face and match it with the familiar voice. The beard was a little whiter, cleanly shaven around the neck, and the hairline on top had receded another inch or two.

'You look different too,' said Grechko, now standing in front of him.

Just for a moment, he smiled.

Dominik took a deep breath as though to catch his heart from falling. He could feel the subtle pressure of tears at the back of his eyes. He rolled his tongue, pushed what saliva he could to the front of his mouth and spat onto Grechko's face.

Grechko briefly touched the spit in his beard before his temper snapped. He threw his hands around Dominik's throat and squeezed to crush it. He struggled with his balance as Dominik pushed himself towards him, aiming kicks between his legs and spitting as much as he could.

Taking a step towards them, Peter raised his gun and brought the butt down as hard as he could onto the back of Dominik's head. Dominik sank to his knees before falling face first to the floor. His eyes were closed and his body was still.

Grechko looked at Peter and Peter waited in silence for an order that did not come. Eventually, he crouched down over Dominik and pressed two fingers into his neck, looking for a pulse. When he felt it, he let out a sigh of relief and threw his gun to the floor.

XLIV

At first nothing would come into focus, as though he was seeing the world through a distorting sheen of water that refused to drain from his eyes. The moment he put any strain on his muscles a dull yet colossal pain throbbed in his head. He squeezed his eyes shut and began to blink. Tears ran down his cheeks as he raised his head in spite of the pain, and his focus became a little sharper. His hands were still locked behind his back but now they were shackled to the frame of the chair in which he sat. Something smothered his mouth, forcing him to breathe solely through his nose. The room was dark but for a patch of light on the ceiling, coming from the street, and quiet but for the sound of running water in the next room.

Dominik sat up as straight as he could and tried to bring the pain in his head under some sort of control. He didn't have to think to recall where he was or how he had come to be there. He knew that before he knew who he was.

The door to the next room opened, flooding the room with light, accentuating the pain in his head. He closed his eyes and turned away from the door. He could hear Russian coming from what he guessed was the bathroom and tried to block his understanding of the words. Then he recognised Grechko's voice, his tone just as coarse as he remembered.

Grechko saw straight away that Dominik was awake. He

took a chair from the corner of the room and placed it in front of him. Dominik slid his foot underneath it and flipped it onto its side. Grechko picked the chair up and placed it back on its legs out of Dominik's reach.

Peter and Konstantin emerged from the bathroom, Peter carrying a bowl in his hands. He set the bowl down next to Grechko's chair. A roll of cotton bandage lay soaking in water. Peter took his gun from his jacket, placed it on a table in the far corner of the room and turned on a lamp. He took a grip of Dominik's neck and pushed his head down between his knees. Blood rushed to Dominik's head, making it throb more than ever. He let out a long, guttural groan. Konstantin cut Dominik's shirt, from the hem up to the collar and down the lengths of both sleeves, until the fabric fell away, leaving his upper body naked.

'Do you remember this one?' Grechko asked, kneeling down at the bowl and slowly lifting the roll of cotton from the water. Peter lifted Dominik into an upright position. 'Before your time, I expect,' said Grechko.

Peter took a grip of Dominik's elbows and raised his arms as high as they would go. Grechko wrapped the bandage tightly around Dominik's chest, yard after yard, encasing it in cotton. Lukewarm water dribbled down his skin and soaked into the tops of his trousers. When he had finished, Grechko took a step back to admire his work. Satisfied with what he saw, he ordered Peter and Konstantin out of the room. Konstantin hesitated for a moment but Peter left the room without looking back.

'What was all that about?' asked Konstantin in the hallway.

They heard the door lock from the inside. Peter shook his head and walked away. He couldn't explain.

Grechko turned to Dominik and smiled. He took off his jacket and threw it onto the nearest chair. He rolled up his sleeves, lit a cigarette and turned off the lamp in the corner. He walked to the window and looked down at the street, casting a shadow onto the ceiling. Dominik tried to stretch his mouth open but the tape held fast.

'Every time I ask myself if you shouldn't warrant my sympathy, I see that young man's face. What was his name?'

He took the seat opposite Dominik and paused as though trying to remember.

'Sean,' he continued. 'Had you forgotten?'

He looked searchingly at Dominik.

'No. I think you remember his name. You wouldn't believe the trouble you caused with that one. No guns, no money, no bloody Irishman. We never found a body, you know. Whoever did that one for you did a good job. If there was one thing I was sure of, it's that you didn't have the stomach for that. Pay someone to do that sort of thing for you. I taught you that myself but...' Grechko stretched himself out for inspection and laughed, 'as you see, I'm a changed man.

I had to find you myself in the end. No one else cared where you were but me. I never understood that. I always wondered where you were. If you thought the price you paid was worth it. If I knew you as well back then as I think I did, I'd say you don't think so. You don't think it was worth it. I bet you've suffered for that. One more year and, who knows? I bet you've thought about that.'

The longer he spoke, the less he looked at Dominik. He focused instead on the smoke rising from his cigarette and tried to remember the things he'd always wanted to know that only Dominik could tell him.

The cotton around Dominik's chest matched the temperature of his skin, so he couldn't feel its touch. He only knew it was there due to the hugging sensation around his chest and the dampness in his lap where the water had dripped.

Grechko stubbed out his cigarette, as though he had suddenly come out of a trance. He shot Dominik a quizzical look.

'Where does Alex come into all of this?' he asked. 'I don't understand any of that.'

Dominik looked up for the first time.

'Ah,' he said quietly, 'now you speak Russian.'

Grechko shuffled to the edge of his chair.

215

'You know, even Dracula had trouble biting the one he loved. All the lies you must have fed him, and yet you still drag him into all of this. You know, he reminds me of you.

When you had a conscience.'

Dominik was trying to listen but his thoughts were beginning to stray. As the bandages around his chest dried the cotton began to contract. The pressure on his lungs was making it harder to breathe. He could feel an increasing ache in his ribs. He filled his lungs as much as he could and blew as hard as he could to clear his nose. Strands of mucus dropped onto his lap but a clear nose made it easier to breathe. He began to take shallower breaths.

'I trust it was quick for the Irishman,' said Grechko.

He sat listening to Dominik's faint breathing and watched the time pass on his watch. A car drove by on the street below. Grechko went to the window to see if it had stopped. He looked out with a glancing interest as a woman came running out of the opposite building, waving to the driver. She climbed into the back seat and the car pulled away again. Grechko stepped back from the window.

He left the room and soon Dominik could hear him in the kitchen, dropping ice into a glass and pouring himself a drink. Dominik swallowed at the thought of liquid and breathed deeper than he'd intended. There was a dull thud beneath the cotton on his chest and a sharp pain channelled through his nerves. The shock made him gasp for air, and he felt two more cracks, both louder than before. He managed to keep himself breathing outwards with a lamenting groan. He kept his breaths shallow again. He looked towards the kitchen to see if he'd been heard. Grechko stood leaning on the frame of the door, watching.

'Do you ever wonder what happened to your father?' he asked.

Dominik stared down at the floor as Grechko took a sip of his drink and walked back to the chair in front of him.

'Of course you do,' he continued. 'I only wish I could tell you, but, to be honest, I never found out. He's not where you think he is, I know that much. I found a record of him being moved east, Norilsk, I think. A year later, your mother tried to register him dead.' He hunched his shoulders. 'What was she thinking?'

Dominik shook his head violently from side to side as though trying to force Grechko's words from his ears.

'No,' he said. 'I don't know either. She must have been out of her mind.'

Dominik looked up from the floor and mumbled a remark that threatened to choke him. Grechko raised his eyebrows.

'What was that?'

He reached across and ripped the tape from Dominik's mouth. Another rib cracked as Dominik gasped for air. He raked up the air from the bottom of his lungs along with everything else that came with it. He pushed himself forward and spat with all the strength he had left.

He stared at Grechko's shirt and what had come from inside of him. Even in the low light he could see the blood that ran every shade of red, pale to almost black. Grechko looked down at his shirt without saying a word. He took the scissors that Konstantin had left on the table and, showing no concern for whether he broke the skin or not, forced one of the blades under the cotton and began to cut it loose. As the cotton fell away from his chest, Dominik gasped for air. With each breath he could feel his splintered ribs scratching at the tissue of his lungs.

Grechko took some more tape from the roll on the table and, despite a token struggle, forced it over Dominik's mouth. It was harder to breathe through his nose and the air didn't feel as clean, but his breaths were easier now that the cotton had gone.

Grechko walked into the bathroom and turned on the light. He removed his shirt and took another look at it before closing the door behind him.

XLV

There was no way of marking the passage of time that night, until the sun rose on a morning Dominik hadn't expected to see. Throughout the night, blood had continued to seep into his lungs, adding a rattle to his breathing. At increasingly regular intervals, he would cough the blood up into his mouth and swallow it down to his stomach. Twice he was sick and he swallowed that too.

He spent most of the night thinking about his breathing, but as exhaustion slowly crept through his body and mind, his thoughts wandered.

He saw the lake past the woods that claimed so many hours of his childhood summers. He had visions of Martina, time and again, who had swum with him. The lake froze in winter, he thought, though not always. Diamonds made of snow that fell from Moscow skies, wet shining pavements that felt slick to the feet, the sliver of rain on his neck, ten steps clear of Charing Cross station.

'You smell of piss,' Grechko said, lifting one of the windows open.

He looked up and down Dominik's body wondering where it would be safe to touch him.

'We'd better do something with you,' he continued. 'We have visitors coming.'

Dominik raised his head. Grechko was wearing a new shirt. How long had all this been planned? Dominik asked himself. How long had it been going on? A pain shot through the back of his neck and, in defeat, he let his chin sink back onto his chest. The more feeble and lifeless he looked, he thought, the more mercy he might be shown.

'Alex made an early start,' said Grechko. 'He'll be coming to see you.'

He walked behind Dominik's chair and unlocked the handcuffs from his wrists. Dominik peeled the tape from his mouth, slid on to his knees and spat onto the floor. There was a dark, even shade of blood.

'Get into the bathroom,' said Grechko.

He was holding a gun by his side, pointed down at the floor. It struck him as quite unnecessary and he put the gun onto the table.

Ignoring his begging pride, Dominik made his way to the bathroom on all fours, crawling slowly. When he got to the toilet he was sick. It hurt more than he could stand. He held on to the seat and cried.

Trying not to move his chest, he slowly stripped and climbed into the bath. Grechko stood at a distance and showered him down with cold water. Dominik lay on his side curled up like a foetus. As vulnerable then as the day he was born.

After a few minutes, Grechko turned the shower off and fetched him some clothes. He lay them next to the sink.

'I'll leave you to dress,' he said. 'They won't be long. I suggest you're quick.'

As he lay shivering in the bath, recovering his breath, he considered the possibility that Alex might be forced to go through all of this himself. The torture, the ritual humiliation. He bowed his head and prayed that Grechko was lying. He wished his own death could be compensation enough for Grechko's grievances. Eventually, he picked himself up and slowly crawled out onto the floor.

A towel lay on top of the clothes by the sink. He stood up

slowly and reached for the towel to dry himself. Beneath the towel lay a dark green uniform, embellished with military frills. He checked the shoulders and sleeves for rank then examined the jacket more closely, until he was sure it was his. The same one he had left hanging in his wardrobe, the day the snow should have covered his tracks.

The bathroom door creaked open and Dominik stood in the doorway, naked, with the uniform in his hands. The sun was high enough now to flood the front room with light and consigning the night gone by to the past. Grechko looked around, checking that nothing looked out of the ordinary. He stared for a moment at his radio on the table and wondered how much longer they would be. Dominik was standing in the doorway.

'Put it on,' said Grechko. 'It's yours, isn't it?'

Dominik took small, agonisingly slow steps towards him and dropped the uniform onto the floor.

'Not any more,' he said, in English, his voice broken beyond recognition by the blood in his lungs.

Grechko stood up tall and flexed his shoulders, as though he could menace him still, or in some way that he hadn't already. A voice crackled over the radio and Dominik lunged for it. Grechko reached the table first but took the gun instead.

'Put the radio down,' Grechko shouted, aiming the gun at Dominik.

He squeezed his eyes shut, as though his vision was the source of all his pain. He threw the radio as hard as he could and yelped when he jerked his ribs. The radio smashed through the window sending a shower of glass out on to the street. They heard it break on the road.

Praying that there might be people on the street, that someone's curiosity might get the better of them, Dominik gripped the back of a chair that was tucked beneath the table and, unable to throw it with his arms alone, swung his body round and aimed again for the window. Grechko blocked its flight, taking the full force of the chair in his back. He fell to one knee. He heard his gun hit the ground but he couldn't see it anywhere.

Dominik collapsed on top of him, dragging him down to the floor. Grechko kicked out, trying to drag himself clear. Catching hold of his trouser leg, Dominik managed to hold Grechko's leg hard enough to stop it from kicking. He bared the skin and bit through the calf as hard as he could. Grechko let out a high-pitched yelp as he felt his flesh tear. He lashed out furiously with his fists, striking the arms that Dominik raised in defence. They both struggled to their feet but Dominik was clumsy and sluggish. His orientation had gone, his fight was slowly dying, and he swayed on his feet like a toddler. He felt Grechko take him by the wrist and heard a guttural roar as he began to spin. The colours in the room became streams of light until his wet skin slipped from Grechko's grip.

The moment seemed frozen to Grechko; the features of Dominik's face distilling, as the light from the window cast them into silhouette, the sound of cracking glass, and his naked body motionless, touched by the warmth of the sun.

A sharp scream from the street below gradually brought Grechko round, like the slow count back from hypnosis. He went to the window. Dominik's body lay sprawled on the roof of a car, broken, lifeless and cold.

XLVI

On their last morning in Dubá, Alex awoke with a sense of happiness. Even before he could recall a reason for the feeling he had to concede that happiness was upon him. He reached out across the bed to touch her. It was more than he could do to leave her be. He pressed his lips against her shoulder and rested them there, absorbing her scent until she eventually opened her eyes. She rubbed them at the corners and enquired about the time.

It was eight o'clock, the earliest they had managed so far together, but neither of them felt like sleeping any more. Over the past few days, time they had spent physically unaware of each other felt like an extravagance. Alex curled his body around Olina's. They lay still and talked until they were both as awake as each other. She wanted to take a walk after breakfast, to find the lake they could see from the window. She had one eye on the walk itself but one eye on a swim. Alex shifted himself up the bed, lifting his shoulders on to the pillows.

'I think we should get back to Prague this morning,' he said.

Olina let out a slow and protesting moan.

'I have to see Dominik for a little while. Sort a few things out.'

'You can't work the Sunday,' she said.

'It's not just work,' replied Alex. 'I really have to see him.'

She propped herself up to face him.

'Neděle,' she said, stressing every syllable. Alex grinned, happy to have understood.

'I know it's Sunday, but I'd like you to meet him too. The sooner the better.'

'I can meet him any time.'

'Lunchtime, then,' Alex said, 'and then the afternoon is ours, I promise.'

He threw back the covers and began to gather his clothes before she had a chance to object.

Things would be easier on all sides, thought Alex, the sooner Dominik and Olina met, but that was a fragment of the truth. He was nervous at the prospect of going back to face Dominik alone. He knew that if Olina were not the first topic, she would be the inevitable destination of their conversation. Her presence would, he hoped, at least force a cordial response from Dominik, if he knew him at all.

They ate a breakfast of bread and ham and packed their things. They were on the road by ten o'clock.

XLVII

From the window where Konstantin was watching them, the streets of Prague were quiet. For this one day of the week, he thought, time was something to be taken rather than raced. Wherever it was they were going, no one seemed in a hurry to get there.

Peter and two other men, one heavy-set and balding, the other wide-eyed and impatient were sitting at the dining table, not far from the window, chatting. The night before, Peter had slept in Dominik's bed, as it was the largest one he could find. The others had arrived first thing in the morning. Konstantin had taken the sofa for the night. It was all the comfort his muddled and erratic conscience would allow him. He couldn't have settled for anything better.

Admiring all the details of the room, its lofty ceilings and handmade furniture, inspired nothing but envy in him. It must be quite a life this Dominik's led, he thought, the kind I could lead myself.

The phone on top of the desk began to ring.

'Don't answer it,' Peter said, an edge of panic in his voice.

Run, Konstantin told himself, answer that phone and tell them not to come. He looked at the others, none of who moved. There might yet be a road to reparation your soul can take, he thought. The phone stopped ringing. Before any of them had time to gather a thought, the radio at Peter's side crackled into life. He listened for a moment.

'He's downstairs,' he announced jumping up from the table.

Konstantin looked out of the window. The black BMW he'd been looking out for all morning was being parked across the street.

'Get back from the window,' snapped Peter. 'Do you know what you're going to say?'

His English was far from perfect but it was the best among them. He assumed it was the only reason he was there. Each of them hid from view of the door and took out their guns, except Konstantin. He sat down at the bottom of the stairs, his gun still holstered beneath his jacket. He couldn't see what difference one more would make.

Olina admired the street while Alex took his bag from the boot of the car.

'If I lived here, maybe I don't mind Prague so much,' she said.

Alex was too preoccupied to reply. He hoped that even though there was no answer on the phone, Dominik might see them on the street. He glanced up at the window but couldn't see anyone there.

The décor in the entrance hall was very much to Olina's taste. The tiles on the walls were clean and bright and the doors and fittings looked new, compared to the rest of the city. Alex called the lift and they rode up to the top in silence. As soon as they stepped inside the flat he called out Dominik's name.

'He pick up phone if he was here,' said Olina. 'We come for nothing.'

'Maybe he's upstairs,' said Alex.

He put his bag down under the hat stand and went to check. There was a man sitting on the steps. Alex recoiled and Konstantin stared up at him, waiting to be addressed.

'Hello,' Alex said, cautiously.

He looked back over to Olina, who smiled at his discovery and walked over to be introduced.

'Těší mě,' she said, extending a hand to whom she assumed was Dominik.

With a glazed expression of remorse Konstantin looked at them both, then placed the palms of his hands slowly on top of his head.

'Please, hands on the head.'

Alex saw Konstantin glancing past him and turned around to see what was there. Peter was aiming his gun at Alex. He cocked the pin of his gun and reset his aim. Olina began screaming as two other armed men appeared from the kitchen and Alex threw up his hands to guard himself.

'Please, please, hands on the head,' Konstantin yelled, jumping up from the stairs and putting himself between Peter and Alex.

'Where's Dominik?' shouted Alex.

'We go see Dominik,' Konstantin replied, as calmly as he could manage. 'But please, hands on the head.'

Slowly, and with their eyes resting on each other, Alex and Olina raised their hands. He shook his head at Olina, trying to communicate his total incomprehension, but he was too scared to talk. Her eyes seemed paralysed.

The two of them were led out of the flat and down to the street where an empty car was waiting. Konstantin drove while Peter sat on the passenger side. He kept his body turned to face Alex and Olina and aimed his gun through the gap in the seats.

'Is that necessary?' asked Konstantin.

Peter answered him with a look and didn't put the gun away.

They crossed Jiráskův Most and then Charles Square. Konstantin could see Olina's face in the rear view mirror, wearing the bewildered expression of the wrongly accused. Alex tried to put an arm around her but she moved along the seat away from him. He glared at Peter, wanting to shift the blame.

'Where is Dominik?' he asked.

Peter crossed his lips with his finger to ask for silence. At Náměsti Miru they turned left into Vinohrady. Two blocks away from the main road Konstantin pulled in to the curb and stopped the engine.

'You should let him know we're here,' he said to Peter, pointing to the radio.

'Hold this.'

Peter passed his gun over to Konstantin. He let it rest on his knees. Peter spoke into the radio and waited for Grechko's orders.

There was a heavy silence while they waited for a response. Peter addressed the radio again and, as he spoke, there was a loud breaking of glass from up above. Grechko's radio shattered on the road. Peter and Konstantin looked at each other in bewilderment.

'What do we do?' asked Konstantin, beginning to panic.

Peter spoke into the radio again.

'It's on the road,' Konstantin shouted, throwing up his hands in disbelief. 'For Christ sakes!'

He forced the gun back into Peter's hand.

Again from above came the sound of breaking glass. Olina screamed, looked away from her window and flung herself into Alex's lap. He covered her with his arms, closed his eyes and bent down to kiss her shoulder. He heard a shower of glass on the pavement, the bending of metal and the sound of someone's breath leave their body. Her skin felt cold on his face and she shook as though she had a fever.

XLVIII

Had the room been any darker Suley would have left the phone to ring. But the weak light of early morning had already broken through his blinds. Since he could see the phone at his bedside he felt inclined to answer it. He checked the incoming number and spoke.

'Do you know what time it is?'

'Six o'clock,' replied Alex.

'Alex!'

Suley tried to shake off the sleepiness and adopt his signature jovial tone.

'I thought you were Dominik. What's the matter?'

'Dominik's dead,' said Alex. 'You know that…don't you?'

'No,' Suley whispered, 'I didn't know that.'

He had nothing to offer Suley along with the news. He had rung for advice and an explanation, not to offer his sympathies. The silence lasted as long as Suley could bear it.

'When did it happen?' he eventually asked.

'Yesterday morning.'

'And you haven't rung me until now? What have you been doing?'

'Hiding,' replied Alex.

Suley took a moment to consider what might have happened but reached no conclusions.

'Jesus,' he said.

His voice was unrecognisable to Alex.

'Where are you?' asked Suley.

'I'm in the park. On Petřín hill.'

'Well, stay there and keep that phone on,' said Suley. 'I'll come and see you.'

As soon as he put down the phone Suley got out of bed. He walked around his flat, reeling up the blinds on the windows, flooding the rooms with as much light as the grey morning could give. He made himself a coffee and settled down by the window in his kitchen. I'll drink this, he told himself, and then I'll get dressed.

XLIX

Alex hadn't slept at all. He had rested once or twice beneath some bushes where he might hear people approach. But the harder he tried to hear the footsteps of people who were not there, the louder he heard them, and with the grass growing wetter as the night went on the prospect of sleep slowly disappeared. He'd waited to phone Suley until all his suspicions had faded, but, when they had failed to do so, he realised he could put his trust in no one else.

Past the tower and beyond the trees where he sat, Petřín Hill descended to the city streets. Dew, and a morning tide of freshly shed autumn leaves adorned the hill. By rights, he said to himself, he and Dominik should be zigzagging their way up the hill in an hour or two. A morning run followed by a day like any other. There was never any harm in that. An afternoon in peace, an evening of each other's company. They could eat at the Fisherman's Club, thought Alex, and, either stay there and drink, or walk on somewhere else. There would be a nice place on Nerudova that he hadn't been to yet, or, maybe cross the river and see what they could find.

He felt worn down by the night but he still kept watch all around him, like a withered one–man garrison. He stared down at the city, and the city stared back at him.

An hour after he had spoken to Alex, Suley arrived at the

park. He found Alex sitting on a bench at the top of the orchard hill. Suley had chosen the black suit from his wardrobe and wore a long dark coat. He walked with his hands in his pockets and his head bowed low. Alex saw him from a distance but didn't greet him. He turned away and sat with his head in his hands until Suley took a seat next to him.

'You look like you're going to a funeral,' said Alex.

'This may be the best I get,' replied Suley. 'Are you going to tell me what happened?'

'I thought you'd already know,' Alex replied, slowly shaking his head in his hands.

'Well, I don't,' said Suley. 'And I don't like to just ask anyone.'

Alex took a deep breath and looked up to the sky as though he expected to find an answer there. Suley stretched out his legs and crossed them at the ankles.

'I was away for the weekend, in Dubá,' said Alex. 'He has a house in the country.'

'I know.'

'I was there with a girl. He didn't know about her but there wasn't much to tell. We came back yesterday to see him and there were men in the flat. They were waiting for us. I don't know who they were, what they wanted, anything. He was missing. They had guns. Fucking guns, Suley!'

Alex's tone demanded some kind of explanation. Suley said nothing.

'They said they were taking us to see him.'

'Where did they take you?' asked Suley.

Alex pointed across the river towards the television tower and looked to Suley.

'Vinohrady. Does that mean anything to you?'

Suley shrugged his shoulders. It would only serve as bitter memory. It meant nothing to him now.

'We stopped on some street. We'd only been there a second and then, she screamed. Nobody did anything. I heard the glass and then...'

Alex stopped. His eyes had been closed when it happened but somehow his memories were visions. He found it impossible to associate them with words.

'What?' Suley asked, coaxing him.

'They threw him out of a window.'

Suley unfolded his legs and re-crossed them again.

'He's dead. I saw him on the car.'

'Are you sure it was him?'

Alex nodded.

'He was naked. I saw his face. He looked black and… blood – Christ, he was covered in blood. I just stood there looking at him. I didn't know what else to do. Olina ran. I don't know if she was running from them or me.'

'What did you do?' asked Suley.

'I ran too, eventually. Some old man came to the window and shouted my name. I didn't know who he was but I ran anyway. I tried looking for her but she was gone. I didn't know what to do. Call you, call the police – I kept thinking to call him. I came here instead. I've been waiting to call you ever since.'

'You think I had something to do with it?'

Alex couldn't answer immediately.

'We argued the last time we spoke,' said Alex.

'So did we,' said Suley.

'What do I do?' He looked Suley in the eye for the first time. 'What do I do now?'

'I don't believe you don't know the answer to that.'

'Well, why don't you tell me?'

'Go home, Alex. Get out of Prague. Whatever you thought you were doing is over.'

Alex stood up and stepped away from the bench. The air was cold and a fine sleet was on the wind. He brushed the moisture into his hair with his hand. He turned to face Suley.

'It isn't over. It's a mess, that's what it is. We've got to sort it out.'

'He's dead, Alex. You say it yourself. How do we sort that out? What do you think I can do?'

He lowered his head and his voice.

'I don't care about them. I cared about him.'

Alex turned away and walked out, towards the edge of the hill.

'I'll do what I can for him. I promise you that.' Suley stood up and walked to Alex's side. 'But I don't want to see you again.'

Suley placed a hand on his shoulder and took an envelope from his coat pocket. He pushed it into Alex's hand.

'This is for you,' he said. 'Go home. Please don't let me see you again.'

Alex opened the envelope and looked inside. Our money looks strange, he thought. There was too much to count and no time to do so. Suley was walking away, his hands back in his pockets. Alex called after him.

'Is that what it comes down to?'

Suley didn't answer and he didn't turn around. The dew on the grass had soaked into his shoes. It felt like grief, pulling down heavy on his heels. He tried very hard not to think about anything.

The envelope was too thick to fit inside his pocket so he held it in his hand. What was it supposed to represent anyway, he asked himself. Compensation for the past? The key to a brighter future?

He wondered how much was there and looked again. Too much to count but more than enough, for London, for anywhere. He knew he would have to leave.

He crouched down to feel the wet of the grass beneath his feet. He had to wait for an idea of what to do. From the top of the hill he could see down to the river, the steep slopes of Vinohrady on the other side, and the hills that lay north and south. This city curves like a bowl, he thought. You are drawn to its centre by gravity.

Acknowledgements

I owe a great deal of thanks to Joanna Scutts, whose efforts and wisdom were so vital to the writing of this book, and I hope, the books to come. To Jenny, I owe everything else.